C0-GHC-664

COULD HE TRUST CASEY?

"Gil?" she said.

He felt Casey's hand touching his hair.

"Yes?"

"We have to go. Our time is running out. Do you think you can get up?"

She sat on the bed by him and then put her arm behind his back and then helped him sit up.

He felt a scream of pain welling to his lips but he fought it back.

He went through the agony of rising up, and all the time her large eyes were tenderly and anxiously upon him.

Are you on my side? he thought.

Or are you still with them?

Playing a savage, devilish game with me . . .

Other Avon Flare Books by
Jay Bennett

THE EXECUTIONER
I NEVER SAID I LOVED YOU
THE PIGEON
SLOWLY, SLOWLY, I RAISE THE GUN

Avon Books are available at special quantity discounts for bulk purchases for sales promotions, premiums, fund raising or educational use. Special books, or book excerpts, can also be created to fit specific needs.

For details write or telephone the office of the Director of Special Markets, Avon Books, Dept. FP, 1790 Broadway, New York, New York 10019, 212-399-1357.

The Death Ticket

Jay Bennett

AN AVON FLARE BOOK

THE DEATH TICKET is an original publication of Avon Books. This work has never before appeared in book form. This work is a novel. Any similarity to actual persons or events is purely coincidental.

AVON BOOKS
A division of
The Hearst Corporation
1790 Broadway
New York, New York 10019

Copyright © 1985 by Jay Bennett
Published by arrangement with the author
Library of Congress Catalog Card Number: 85-90656
ISBN: 0-380-89597-8

All rights reserved, which includes the right to reproduce this book or portions thereof in any form whatsoever except as provided by the U. S. Copyright Law. For information address Literistic Ltd., 264 Fifth Avenue, New York, New York 10001.

First Flare Printing, October 1985

FLARE TRADEMARK REG. U. S. PAT. OFF. AND IN OTHER COUNTRIES, MARCA REGISTRADA, HECHO EN U. S. A.

Printed in the U. S. A.

K-R 10 9 8 7 6 5 4 3

For Mae,
Dearly loved and sadly missed

THE DEATH TICKET

1

He remembered that it all started with the wind, a gray autumnal wind that blew all morning, into the afternoon and then slowly, softly began to let up with the coming of dark evening. Yet it still blew against the windows of the small wooden house, and sitting in his room just under the peaked roof, he could hear it, all the time.

He looked up from his book, listening to it, ever listening to it, the light of the lamp shadowing his pale face.

Within him was a great searching silence.

And then the bell rang.

The sound floated up to him, thin but clear. It seemed to waken faint echoes in the darkening empty house.

He got up from his chair, set his book down on the little desk, and then slowly went down the steps. As he did, the ringing became louder and more insistent, for some reason making his hands tremble just a bit.

And he couldn't understand that.

He came to the locked door and looked through the dim fanlight and out onto the porch. He saw a grayish-blue figure with a hat that had a visor that shone bleakly in the fading light.

He turned the lock and opened the door.

"Yes?"

The wind entered the house, softly.

"I've got a letter for Gilbert Ward."

"I'm Gil Ward."

He looked at the lean, hard face of the mailman. He had never seen him before. Gil knew all the mailmen in his small town.

"It's special delivery and registered."

"Oh."

"You'll have to sign for it."

"All right."

The man had a hard, dry voice. The eyes were sharp and piercing.

"You sign here."

He pointed a lean, long finger.

"Sure."

Gil signed his name and the man handed him the letter.

"Hope it's good news."

But there was an ironic edge to his voice.

"Hope so," Gil said.

The man still stood there. Beyond him was the darkening sky. Night will soon come down, Gil thought. The sun is long gone.

Then he heard the man's voice.

"You've never seen me before, have you?"

"No," Gil said.

"How long you live here in Bolton?"

"All my life."

"How long is that?"

"Seventeen years."

The piercing eyes swept over Gil. The visor glinted.

"You look older."

"Maybe because I'm tall," Gil said.

The letter felt cold in his hand.

"Maybe so. I'm helping out. I'm from Midwood Post Office."

Midwood was two towns away. On the Connecticut border.

"Oh," Gil said.

But he didn't believe him. And he didn't know why.

"You're my last stop and then I'm going home."

Gil didn't say anything.

"You live alone here?"

"No," Gil said.

"I do. I'm a loner."

I guess you are, Gil thought. It's in your eyes. And your face.

"All my life. You look like a loner, too," the man said.

Gil didn't answer him.

"It's like a disease. You catch it young and it stays with you all your life. No cure for it."

The voice was sad and haunting, yet the eyes were direct and penetrating, always studying Gil.

"Who do you live with here?"

"My aunt and uncle," Gil said.

"What do they do?"

"They run the drug store in town."

"Rogers Pharmacy?"

"That's it."

"No parents?"

"No."

"Dead?"

"That's about it," Gil said.

"Hope it's good news," the man said.

"Uh-huh."

"I carry a lot of bad news these days. I can see it in the people's faces when they get the letter."

"I guess you do."

The man stood there silent and Gil waited for him to go.

"Winter will be here soon."

"It's on its way," Gil said.

"Think it'll be a cold one?"

"Looks like it."

"How do you know?"

"Just feel it."

The man looked up at the sky and nodded his head bitterly. The visor glinted and flashed in the last light of the fading day.

"I guess you're right. A cold and bleak one. I'll freeze again."

The old tree in the front yard rustled quietly. A car passed down the shaded lane and then everything was silent as before.

Silent and darkening.

Gil heard the man's voice again.

"We're so close to the City. Just forty miles away from New York City and yet we get such harsh winters."

"That's how it is."

"Could be living up in Maine. How do you figure that one out?"

"Haven't yet," Gil said.

The man leaned forward to him, his face suddenly angry and tense.

"You go to high school."

"So?"

"Science courses. You take science courses. Biology, physics, all that crazy, intricate stuff."

"I take biology. It's not crazy."

"Then you should know the answers."

Gil shook his head.

"No answers," Gil said.

"No answers," the man echoed. "Today nobody has answers. Only questions. That's all you hear are questions. We're scared people. The night's coming down over all of us. We're going to be blown away. You ever think of that?"

"Sometimes I do," Gil said quietly.

The tree in the front yard rustled again. There were no leaves on its old, worn branches.

The wind had long since blown them away.

"Cain killed Abel. Man was always a killer. And there's nothing you can do about it. Nothing."

"If that's the way you see it."

"That's the way I see it, young fellow."

Then the fire went out of the man's eyes. He pointed to the letter.

"Hope it's good news."

You don't, Gil thought.

"Good talking to you. I'm a lonely person. I told you that."

"Yes," Gil said.

"I told you that," the man repeated.

Without another word, he turned away abruptly.

Gil watched him go down the porch steps, across the dusty path and then into his car. He waited for the car to start up and go off down the lane, and when it was out of sight he turned and closed the door and locked it.

The house seemed very quiet to him.

Quiet and strange.

He stood for a moment, listening to the soft wind against the windows.

"Never saw him before," he said low.

But his voice sounded loud and hollow in the empty house.

"Never."

He went up the stairs, slowly and thoughtfully, the letter gripped tight in his hand.

"Never saw him around Midwood, either."

When he got to his room he dropped the letter onto his desk and sat down. The letter gleamed white under the small yellow lamp.

Gil's shadow was over the wall, long and angular.

He sat there a long time, still hearing the man on the porch, and still seeing him standing there, tall and lean and hard, the eyes suddenly going strange with a deep and wild light in them, the coming night, like a dark mantle, hovering over both of them.

Finally, he stirred and picked up the letter and glanced at the writing on the envelope.

He had no expression on his face.

He knew the handwriting.

Knew it well.

Gil opened the envelope and took out a short note. It was written in a large, scrawling hand, the same as on the envelope.

Large, uneven letters.

Gil,

Take care of this for me. Take good care of it,

The Dwarf

He put his hand into the envelope and took out the half of a New York State lottery ticket.

It was this week's ticket.

He read the numbers.

25-30-32.

He smiled sadly to himself.

"Always half a ticket. Always the same numbers. It's a ritual with him."

He wondered who had the other half of the ticket. And what numbers were on that half.

But then he said to himself, It doesn't really matter. They could all be zeros. He never wins anyway. Doesn't even come close.

Just gets his hopes and dreams up for nothing.

Like millions of other lonely and wounded people.

All losers.

The Dwarf is no different.

This ticket is no different.

This wounded ticket.

Gil sighed low and got up and went to his bed. He got down to his knees and then drew out from under the bed a small metal box.

It was made of brass and it had the figure of a frog with bulging eyes embossed on its top.

Gil's hand traced over the figure of the glinting frog and lingered there gently. Then his fingers came away from it.

He gave it to me on my twelfth birthday, Gil thought.

It'll bring you luck, Gil.

Thanks, Gareth.

We all need luck in this miserable world of ours.

Yes, Gareth. Thanks again. It's beautiful.

Beautiful?

It is.

And the word *beautiful* seemed to make Gareth's eyes glitter and burn. He turned on Gil and shook his head fiercely.

Don't ever call me Gareth again.

But why?

Just don't do it.

It's your name.

I'm sick of it. You call me the Dwarf. Like everybody else does.

I'd rather not.

Do it. I tell you to do it. I'm sick of the lie.

It's not a lie.

It is. Look at me and tell me that it isn't a dirty lie. Look at me.

There was such aching bitterness in his voice and eyes that it made Gil tremble. He even felt like crying and he was ashamed of that.

You call me the Dwarf. That's exactly what I am.

I won't.

You will. Gareth was a knight in King Arthur's court. Do I look like a knight? Tell me. Do I?

His voice was almost a shout.

Gil could not speak.

I look more like King Arthur's jester. The court freak. That's what I look like. A freak.

Not to me.

That's what I am.

No, Gareth.

Don't ever call me that again. Ever.

He turned and left Gil standing alone and desolate.

I never did, Gil thought sadly.

Never after that time.

The wind blew softly against the windows of the room

as Gil opened the box and put the new stub away with the other halves of lottery tickets the Dwarf had sent him over the past year.

He closed the box and his fingers again traced the outlines of the embossed figure, and as they did he thought of the fairy tale about the ugly frog who turns into a handsome prince.

Not in this world.

Only in fairy tales, he said to himself.

Then he slowly closed the box again and pushed it under the bed, deep into the darkness.

But he didn't realize as he rose again to his feet that the half of this ticket was different from all the other halves.

So very different.

For this one carried death with it.

2

He dreamed that night.

He dreamed that he had turned into the Dwarf and the Dwarf had become Gil Ward. The Dwarf was no longer short, of midget height, with a large head, dark curly black hair, a large-featured face, and a raspy voice, but had become a tall, blond, fair-skinned, broad-shouldered and fine-featured person.

Tall, elegant and handsome like a story book prince.

Walked up and down, so very gracefully before Gil, who was now of midget height and who knew with a chilling sense of terror that his features had become large and almost coarse, and that his voice was now low and harsh and unpleasant for anyone to hear.

I've become the Dwarf, he whispered to himself.

He said it again, in terror and despair.

I'm trapped inside his body. I'll never get out again.

And this time he felt shame.

I'll be this way forever now, he thought frantically.

Then his heart began to pound like a great hammer and he tried to scream for help, for someone to come and save him, but no sound would come to his lips. No sound at all.

Within him he was screaming.

All the time.

The prince stopped his strolling, paused before Gil and looked down at him. Then he said scornfully, "And now how does it feel to be the Dwarf?"

Gil put his little hand up pleadingly to the prince, but the prince slapped it away smartly and laughed.

Then he spoke.

"Now just see what it means to walk in this kind and gentle world of ours as a Dwarf. Just try it on for size."

"Please help me."

"Why?"

"Because . . ."

And Gil's voice trailed off into hopelessness.

"Well?"

"Please," he said again to the prince.

"Never."

"But I'm your brother."

"My brother?"

"Yes. I'm your younger brother Gil."

"Impossible. You're a dwarf. How can a prince have a dwarf for a brother? Absolutely impossible and completely unjust. It's just never done."

The prince began to laugh, so loudly that the sound filled Gil's ears like the roar of ocean water. He screamed with pain and fear and this time his voice did come to his lips.

He awoke to the sound of his screaming.

And when he did he saw his Aunt Edith standing in the room, just over the dark threshold.

She had a blue robe over her nightgown and her face was white and dim in the heavy darkness.

"Gil?"

He didn't speak.

"Gil? Are you all right?"

She came over to him.

"Yes," he said in a very low voice.

His voice sounded strange and distant to him.

"You cried out in your sleep. A few times."

"I know."

"You woke me."

"I'm sorry, Aunt Edith."

She sat down on the bed by him.

"Shall I turn on the light?"

"Please."

The light cut into the darkness and threw it back till it hovered in the corners of the room.

The silent corners.

"That better now?"

He nodded, not speaking. He was drenched with perspiration.

Cold and damp.

"Didn't mean to wake you," he said.

"That's all right."

He could hear the wind softly against the windows.

"Did I wake Uncle Joe?"

She shook her head.

"No. He's too tired out."

He's always tired out, Gil thought sadly. Even when I help him out in the store, he still has too much to do.

"I was dreaming," Gil said.

"The same one?"

Then they both were silent.

"He's no good," she finally said in a gentle voice. "Even when he's out of the house he still brings misery and sorrow."

"I wish you wouldn't say that, Aunt Edith."

She looked over to him and then put her hand on his shoulder.

"I'm sorry, Gil."

"He's my brother."

"He's your brother," she said and a tightness had come into her face.

He knew what she was thinking of. He's your brother, and there's nothing you or I or anybody else can do about it.

Fate made him your brother.

But he's evil.

An evil Dwarf.

That's how she often referred to him.

"He's the only one I have," Gil said. "It's just me and the Dwarf."

"I know."

"Uncle Joe always got along with him."

"Joe?"

She was patting her hair down when she said that. Now she drew her hand away and waved it in a tired gesture.

"Joe gets along with everybody. That's how he is."

"He's a fine man."

"True. Too fine a man for this town, Gil. Everybody takes advantage of him. If I weren't around we'd have been on welfare a long time ago. Without store or home."

And he thought, it's so. Aunt Edith was the spine of the household. It was she who took the two of them in when their mother died and their father ran off never to be found again.

It was Aunt Edith who always said the Dwarf took after their worthless father. Gil after her sister, their mother.

You're your mother's image, Gil. I see her every time I look at you.

All you have from your father is his height. Gareth has everything else that man had to give. And it was all bad.

He heard his aunt speaking again.

". . . your mother had such great hopes for Gareth. That was before he was born. That's when she named him. He was to be her first. And she was full of dreams. And then when she saw what she had gotten, it broke her heart."

"That's not so. She loved him. Even more than me."

His aunt's eyes flashed.

"Never more than you, Gil. Never that. She loved him because she was your mother. That's the kind of woman she was. But it broke her heart just the same. I know that and you know that."

"He's my brother," Gil said stubbornly. "My older brother."

"Older? He's no one to look up to."

"But . . ."

"One should be able to look up to an older brother. I always did to mine. And it was right that I should. But Gareth?"

Her voice had tightened as she said the name.

"What did he ever do wrong? You're always down on him. Always. And it's not fair. Not fair at all."

She didn't answer him.

"He's just like other people. But nobody sees that. Nobody."

She shook her head grimly.

"You don't see him as I do. He's mean-spirited. I tell you he's mean. And sooner or later he'll bring great trouble to you, Gil."

Gil turned away from her and looked to the dark window.

He heard her sigh.

"I'm sorry, Gil. I came in to soothe you and I'm just making you feel worse. I know I . . . I . . ."

Her voice trailed off.

"That's all right," he said without turning back to her.

"Forgive me."

"Nothing to forgive."

"There is."

"Nothing," he said again.

She shook her head desperately.

"It's my fault."

"No."

He was still looking at the window and not at her.

"It is. We get onto Gareth and every time it begins the same and ends the same. I shouldn't let it happen that way."

"We'll always talk about him," Gil said.

"Yes," she murmured.

Then neither spoke for a while.

"I think I can sleep now," he said finally.

"Are you sure?"

"Yes."

He had turned back to her.

"Good."

But the two felt that the Dwarf had come in between them.

It always happened that way.

Gil was sure that he was standing in one of the silent, dark corners of the room.

His coal black eyes staring at both of them.

Staring through the darkness.

With hatred and bitterness.

"I'm sorry for what I said about Gareth," she murmured. "I just can't help myself, Gil. I just can't."

"I know."

"I loved your mother very much, Gil."

I loved her, too, he thought.

And even that father of mine, that dim and distant father who beat it out of our lives so clean and so fast.

Like a thief.

Not taking a penny with him. But so much else that was so valuable to our lives.

So much that the Dwarf and I needed.

Especially the Dwarf.

"I had no children, Gil. You know how much I care for you."

"I know," he said.

He thought he could see tears in her eyes. But he wasn't sure.

"I tried so hard with Gareth."

"Yes."

She leaned forward to him and now he could see the tears glisten.

"Believe me, Gil, I did. You don't know that. You don't."

"I guess you did," he said.

She stroked his head tenderly and then she got up and turned out the light.

"Try and sleep now."

"Okay."

She walked noiselessly to the threshold of the room, paused and looked back at him.

He could barely see her dim figure.

"Don't dream anymore."

"I won't."

Then she turned and was gone without a sound.

Leaving him alone.

Completely alone.

With the Dwarf standing in the dark and silent corner.

3

He remembered how it happened. How the first pale shadow of death began to fall slowly over him.

Slowly and surely.

He didn't know it then.

But it was then that it happened.

"Mind if I put the television on, Uncle Joe?"

"Not at all, Gil."

"You sure?"

"Go ahead, Boy."

They were in the back of the store, checking on the stock. It was just before closing time and Aunt Edith was in the front getting things ready for lockup.

They could hear her counting the money in the cash register, the coins dropping into the little compartments.

Dropping with a harsh, metallic sound.

It had been a slow night.

Gil turned on the small set, its volume low, and then he got the channel he wanted.

"Just for a few minutes."

"The lottery?"

"Uh-huh. They're going to give the winning numbers."

"Was going to turn it on myself."

"Why? Do you play it?"

His uncle smiled.

"Every now and then. This one's for six million. Thought I'd take a try at it. How about you?"

"I put a dollar on this one," Gil said.

Gil didn't like lying to his uncle. But he didn't want to tell him that he was looking just to see how the Dwarf made out.

How he lost again.

As he always did.

Joe would understand and yet Gil could hear him say gently, He's all right. But just the same don't get too involved with him. He's all right, Gil, and I mean what I say. But I have a feeling about Gareth. Maybe it's the way he lives there in the City all alone in that loft. I don't know for the life of me what he does to make a dollar. Maybe plays the horses all the time. I hope it's that and nothing worse. I don't know how he pays his rent and eats. I once offered him some spare money I had, a few hundred dollars, and he just walked away from me. That's all in his favor. And yet it's a feeling I have about him, Gil. And we have to trust our feelings if we're decent people. So don't get too involved with him. You understand that, don't you, Gil? Sure you do, son.

"You haven't told your aunt you're playing, have you, Gil?"

Gil shook his head.

"No."

"Neither have I." His uncle smiled.

He was a tall, slender man with graying hair and a worn, worried face. He was much older than his wife. They had both married late. Edith had never had a husband and he had lost his wife just two years before.

The marriage had turned out to be a good one for both of them.

"Better get ready, Gil. Here they come."

"Right."

"Where's your ticket?"

His uncle already had his in his hand.

"Oh, I left it home. But I remember the numbers."

"Here they are. For six million dollars, Gil."

"Six million," Gil said.

"Can do an awful lot with that money."

"Sure can."

"Get six numbers right and you get the jackpot. I'll be able to send you to medical school. Make a doctor out of you. Like you always wanted, Gil."

"First you buy Aunt Edith her new house."

"Right. First thing I'll do. I'll just lift up that phone and call Ed Bailey and buy it. The one on Elmore Street that she has her heart set on."

"Then you close this store and you go around the world with her."

"You have it."

Then they were silent.

They watched the numbers flash onto the screen, listening to the voice as it called them out.

One by one.

Gil's uncle wrote them down on his pad.

Gil just stood there looking at the screen.

Feeling himself go cold all over.

25-30-32 . . .

The Dwarf's numbers.

Gil did not even hear or see the other numbers as they flashed onto the screen.

25-30-32 . . .

"Haven't got a single one of them. No, here's a 38. I got that one, Gil. And a 41. Big deal."

25-30-32 . . .

He watched his uncle take his ticket, tear it up and then drop the bits into the wastebasket.

"A washout. Me and millions of others. Left empty."

Gil couldn't speak.

His uncle turned off the set and turned to him.

"How did you make out?"

"What?"

"With your ticket?"

"Mine?"

"You said you bought a ticket."

"Oh. Yes, I did. I did."

"Well?"

Gil shook his head.

"Nothing. Like you. Not even one number."

"I got two of them."

"You did."

"That's right."

"Two. That's very good."

His uncle stared at him.

"Very good. What's good about getting two numbers?"

"That's right. It doesn't mean a thing."

And then he said to himself, three numbers don't mean a thing. You have to get all six.

Each and every one of the six.

"You're acting strange tonight, Gil."

It is a strange night, Gil thought.

"Anything wrong, son?"

His uncle was looking at him with narrowed eyes.

Gil shook his head.

"No, Uncle Joe. Everything's fine."

"You sure?"

"Yes. Just fine."

But something deep inside of him told him that he was lying to his uncle again.

4

25-30-32.

The Dwarf had hit on all three numbers.

Right on the head.

In deadly sequence.

But what were the numbers on the other half of the ticket?

How did they come out?

How?

He found that out two days later when he was alone in the house and the telephone rang.

He stood listening to it.

Cutting through the stillness like a shining knife.

Shining and cold.

He went down the steps and into the hall and picked up the receiver.

"Hello?"

"Gil?"

It was the Dwarf.

"It's me."

"You alone?"

"Yes."

"They're in town?"

"Yes."

He was waiting, waiting for the Dwarf to speak again.

"Now listen. Listen hard."

He felt his heart tighten.

"Okay."

"That ticket I sent you. That half-ticket."

"Yes?"

"You have it, haven't you?"

"Right."

"Where is it now?"

"In that box you once gave me."

"What box?"

"Don't you remember? The box with the frog on the top and the . . ."

The Dwarf cut in harshly.

"I remember. Now listen."

"Go ahead."

"You take the box with the ticket in it. And you make sure that nobody sees you. Nobody. Do you hear me?"

"Nobody will see me."

"Make sure, I tell you."

"Nobody will see me," Gil said again.

His hand holding the receiver began to shake.

"Better do it tonight. Before they come back from the store."

"Okay."

Gil took a deep breath and then he heard his brother speak again.

"You go down to that old elm tree. The one at the end of the lane. You know which one I mean?"

"Yes."

"Just by the old Mansfield barn. That one."

"I know."

"Good."

Then there was a silence and Gil looked through the window and out at the waning afternoon.

The sky was gray and low. The wind was shaking the branches of the trees. The leafless branches.

In the distance he could see a lone bird, white against

the gray clouds. He watched it with a strange fascination till it finally disappeared from his view.

The Dwarf began speaking again.

As if until then, he, too, had been watching the bird and the gray clouds.

Watching with the same strange fascination until the bird was blotted out by the cruel and enormous sky.

"You pick out a spot near the tree and you dig a little hole and then you put the box in it and cover up the hole. Cover it up good. So nobody can ever tell what you did. Got it?"

Gil didn't say anything.

"You there?"

"Yes, Dwarf. I'm here."

"You heard me?"

"Every word."

"You sure?"

"Yes."

"Now, you got this all straight, Gil?"

"Everything."

"Then you keep put till you hear from me again. Goodbye."

"Dwarf."

"Well?"

"Why am I doing this?"

"Why?"

"Please tell me."

"Sure, I'll tell you."

There was a tantalizing silence and he waited and was about to speak again when he heard the Dwarf's harsh voice.

"Because that ticket is worth one half of six million dollars. That's why."

Gil held the black receiver tight in his grip.

"Three million of that six is mine, Gil. All mine."

"And the other three million?"

"Belongs to Gordie."

"Gordie?"

"A friend of mine. A long-time friend."

There was a slight pause.

"Why am I hiding it?" Gil asked.

"Because Gordie and I have something to straighten out between us. That's why."

"But . . . ?"

"You ask too many questions. Do what I tell you to do."

And then Gil heard the phone click.

"Dwarf."

But there was silence.

Total, eerie silence.

He sat there a long while, staring at the wall. On his forehead were drops of gleaming sweat.

The palms of his hands were moist.

Three million dollars.

It all belongs to the Dwarf.

To my brother, the Dwarf.

He went slowly upstairs to his room, closed the door tight and then walked over to his bed and got down on his knees and reached into the darkness underneath the bed and pulled out the brass box.

The bulging eyes of the frog seemed to glitter at him.

He opened the box and took out the last half-ticket.

25-30-32.

Three million dollars.

"I'm looking at three million dollars," he whispered.

And he felt a cold wind go over him.

He dumped the other half-tickets onto the floor and just left the winning ticket in the box.

Only that.

Then he closed the box and pushed it under the bed again. Back into the darkness.

I'll slip out tonight, while they're asleep, he said to himself.

Tonight.

And he felt the cold wind go over him.

He shivered.

5

He went down the dark deserted lane, the little box tight in his right hand. In his other hand he carried a short-handled digging shovel.

It was well past midnight.

The wind rustled through the trees as he walked. A low, sighing wind.

The stars were few, a sprinkling few.

High, very high in an arcing black sky.

He walked slowly, deliberately, and every twenty yards or so, he would pause and look about him and listen, with all of his senses alert and sharp.

His body tensing for the slightest sound.

But he saw and heard nothing.

Nothing but the sighing wind.

For he was alone.

Completely alone.

He walked on and suddenly he saw a form come gliding out of the darkness toward him and he began to tremble.

The form was low, as if on its knees, and it had two fiery eyes.

He stopped stock-still.

His shovel raised.

The box gripped tight in his right hand.

The form approached and then slid by him and went on down the lane and he saw that it was a dog—one of his neighbor's dogs.

He let out his breath.

"I've got to get hold of myself," he whispered. "I've got to."

But as he walked the tension would not leave him.

Not for an instant.

Just as he neared the old Mansfield barn he heard the distant sound of a car. He stood and listened to it gradually coming closer. Ever closer. He couldn't move. He stood pinned to the spot, watching the two onrushing headlights. They loomed through the darkness like two great shining eyes.

Suddenly he tore himself loose and ran swiftly behind a large tree and stood there.

Still and rigid.

Until the car sped by and disappeared into the night.

Its red taillights vanishing last.

All was quiet again.

Deathly quiet.

He clenched the precious box even tighter and began walking again. And the only sound was the sound of his feet upon the gravel road, one after the other.

One foot after the other.

In deadly rhythm.

Soon the old barn loomed up before him.

Old and misshapen.

He paused and then turned away from it and began to approach the tree. The elm tree. It now stood tall and threatening.

He stopped in front of it.

And he remembered how he and the Dwarf used to sit at the base of the tree in the glowing sunshine and talk away the hours.

Just the two of them.

I was so young then and it was so long ago, he said to himself.

He stood there peering through the night at the tree and it seemed to be staring down at him with a cold anger.

It seemed to be speaking to him.

In the low, low voice of the wind.

His hands trembled and he could almost hear the tree say to him, What are you doing here on this dark, dark night?

What, Gil?

What is the black purpose of that shovel and that box that you carry so desperately in your hand?

That glittering box.

What is going on, Gil?

What murder are you planning?

What body are you hiding?

Listen to me. The Dwarf, your brother, is an evil dwarf.

He has become evil, I tell you.

Your aunt is right, you young fool.

She knows life better than you.

Listen to her.

Turn around and go back.

And suddenly Gil felt an overwhelming weariness come over him. A weariness and a despair.

As if he had been walking mile after mile through a never-ending night.

He could not bear to look at the tree anymore.

Nor hear its voice.

He turned away from it and then looked eagerly, frantically up the lane, way, way back, till he could see a brief stab of light in the blackness that was now all about him.

The light came from a small lamp that stood in the living room window of his house.

His aunt always kept a small light on, all through the night.

He once asked her why she did that, but she would not tell him.

"Just like having it on, Gil."

"But why?"

Her eyes had a distant and strange look to them.

"Just that," she said.

Then he went to his uncle.

"I don't know why," Joe said. "But she has her reasons. Your Aunt Edith always has her reasons. And they're generally good ones."

Now the glimpse of the steady light and the remembered sound of his uncle's gentle voice and the look in the wise eyes seemed to calm and comfort Gil.

He breathed out low and turned away from the lane and back to the grim tree. His lips were set in a thin, determined line as he set down the shovel and the box. Then he reached into the deep pocket of his windbreaker and took out a flashlight and turned it on.

He let the light play on the silent tree and its silent branches and then he swung it over to the old barn.

It stood there, quiet and eyeless.

Its windows long gone. The roof sagging and ready, ever ready, to fall to the ground with a hopeless groan.

For some reason, Gil thought of an old swayback farmhorse, old and worn out and ready to die.

To die.

Then he drove the thought away from him and turned back to the elm tree.

"All right," he murmured. "Let's go."

He searched about till he found a good spot for digging. Then he propped the flashlight upon a rock and began to dig.

The sound of the blade of the shovel as it bit into the hard earth was loud to him.

It brought back all his tensions and fears.

In a hot rush.

"I'd better get this done fast," he said in a low voice. "Get it done and then go."

He stopped only once to catch his breath and to listen. But the night was still and vast about him.

"Nothing," he muttered.

Then he went on with his relentless digging.

And all the while the wind was sighing in the branches of the tree above him. The quiet leafless branches.

Soon he felt that he had gone deep enough.

"Okay."

He knelt and smoothed away the dirt with his hands. Then he took the box and laid it into the hole.

Gently, he said to himself.

Ever so gently.

I'm hiding three million dollars.

A cool three million.

Then he began to cover the box with the soft dirt that lay on either side of the hole.

He stopped for an instant.

To look sharply about and to listen, all of his senses taut.

But he was alone in the night.

Alone.

Far in the distance he suddenly heard the thin bark of a dog. He stood motionless and listened till the sound faded and died.

He turned back to the grim tree.

The last thing that he saw before he had completely covered the box was the glittering eyes of the frog.

Then the earth blotted them out.

6

He had just gotten back into bed and pulled the covers over him when he heard the hushed footsteps of his aunt approach the threshold of his room.

He closed his eyes and pretended to be sleeping.

Then he heard the footsteps come to a stop and he knew that she was standing there, silent in the darkness.

A white dim shape.

"Gil?"

It was said in a low and tender whisper.

He opened his eyes.

"Yes?"

"I didn't mean to wake you. I was just saying your name to myself."

"Oh."

She came through the darkness to him.

"I'm sorry."

"It's all right."

Their voices were low and intimate.

"I had the strangest feeling, Gil. It woke me up and I had to come here."

He waited.

"I had the feeling that you had gone out of the house and . . . and . . ."

Her voice trailed off into the silence.

"Gone out?"

And he wondered if she knew.

"The strangest feeling. Chilled me. That you had gone out of the house and didn't come back."

He didn't speak.

"I trembled, Gil. Just trembled at the thought of it."

"I've been here all the time," he said.

"I know. I know."

"All the time," he murmured.

He thought to himself, I'm lying again.

The Dwarf has me lying.

I've never done this before to them.

Never.

She sat down on the bed and they didn't speak for a while. The wind brushed softly against the windows.

He listened to it and he thought of the box lying in the cold earth with the wind blowing over it.

He heard her voice.

"Don't ever go off and leave me alone, Gil."

"What do you mean?"

"Don't do it, Gil."

She touched his face and her hand was cold.

Cold and shaking.

"Don't go off and leave me here like Gareth did."

He looked at her in astonishment.

"Please don't."

He remembered how he had come home from school one sunny afternoon and Gareth was gone.

The Dwarf was gone.

Never to come back to the house again.

He never knew why.

"You're all I have, Gil. Joe is my husband. But you're my son."

"I'm not going anywhere, Aunt Edith."

"I sound so foolish. But I had such a strange feeling, Gil. So strange and frightening."

"I'll be around a long time," he said.

But her fear had entered into his being and settled there.

Something is taking me away from you, he thought.

Something I have no control over.

And I am getting so scared, Aunt Edith. So very scared.

"Don't leave me, Gil. It's terrible to be alone. So bleak."

"I know," he said gently.

She bent forward to him.

"I . . . I didn't mean to say you're my son. It . . . it just came out of me."

"I like it that way," he said. "I'm glad you called me that."

She pressed his hand and didn't speak.

After a while she rose and went silently out of the room.

7

He sat in the living room, waiting for the call.

And all the time he thought of the Dwarf and the money.

Why did he have me bury the ticket?

Why didn't he just go and collect his three million?

They're waiting to give it to him. The newspapers say there is only one winner of the six million dollars. It has to be him and Gordie.

Gordie has the other winning numbers.

So why don't they get the money?

What's going on between them?

What is there to straighten out?

There is something about this all that makes me shiver. The Dwarf is into a deal that will turn out bad.

I can feel it deep inside of me.

It has to turn out bad.

And I shouldn't be a part of it.

I shouldn't.

Gil got up and began to walk about the silent room, his face white and tense, his lips tight.

He ran his hand through his blond hair and sighed.

I'm getting all worked up about nothing. So I buried the ticket. But that's how the Dwarf is. He's suspicious of the world.

Always was.

Because the world made him that way.

He'll call me and tell me to dig out the box and then he'll come up here and get his ticket and collect his three million.

That's how it's going to be.

I should have more faith in him.

Everybody gives him a bum rap. And I'm beginning to look at him like everybody else does.

I shouldn't. He's my brother and I . . .

Gil frowned.

My brother. And yet how much have we seen each other in the past three years? It's mostly phone calls and the half-tickets he sends me like a ritual every week.

He's my older brother, just the same.

And I should never forget that.

A sad and worried look came into Gil's gray eyes as he sat down and waited for the call that he knew must come.

Toward evening, when the sky was beginning to darken, he heard the ring of the phone.

Cold and distinct.

He went to it and picked up the receiver.

"Hello?"

"It's the Dwarf."

He began to tremble at the sound of the harsh voice. And he said to himself again, it's my brother.

Why do I tremble?

Why?

Then he heard the harsh voice again.

"You did it?"

"Yes, Dwarf."

"Nobody saw you?"

"Nobody."

"You sure now?"

"Yes."

"How far from the tree?"

"I measured off ten feet."

"Ten? That's a lucky number. A Gypsy once told me

that. Ten's a lucky number. But I never played it. What do you think of that, Gil?''

He could hear the Dwarf laugh, a low, almost mocking laugh.

He waited for the laugh to die away.

He felt cold inside of him.

''And then you buried the box, Gil?''

''That's right.''

''The ticket in it.''

''Yes.''

''You covered up the hole good so nobody would ever know you dug there?''

''Nobody ever goes there anyway, Dwarf. You know that.''

''Answer me.''

The voice was taut and harsh.

''I covered it up. Nobody will ever know.''

''Good boy.''

There was a pause.

Gil looked to the window. The sun, the late autumn sun, was slowly falling against a blackening sky.

The bare branches of the trees glowed.

He turned back to the phone at the sound of his brother's voice.

''Where are they now?''

''Who?''

''The aunt and the uncle.''

''Oh. They're in the store. You know that.''

''They never change. In the store.''

''They have to make a living, don't they?''

''Don't they ever go to see a movie?''

''Sometimes.''

''Sometimes.''

There was a pause.

Then he heard the Dwarf's voice again.

''How's business with them?''

''Not so good.''

"The whole town's not so good. So they can use some money?"

"Yes. They sure can."

"Maybe I'll throw them a million or so."

"Cut it out, Dwarf," Gil said.

"Why, what's wrong?"

"You know what's wrong. Stop playing around with me."

"I'm not, Gil. I'm serious about giving them money."

"You're not."

"Then maybe I'm not."

He heard the Dwarf's low mocking laugh. And he could almost see the bitter black eyes.

You shouldn't hate them so, Gil thought to himself.

You really shouldn't.

Joe cares for you. And underneath it all, Aunt Edith has kind feelings for you. I know that she does.

They're two good people.

You have too much hate in you, Dwarf.

It's like a fire inside you. Burning you away.

He heard the Dwarf speak again.

"Then I'll throw them five hundred thousand. In dollar bills. How's that? Does it sit well with you?"

Gil gripped the receiver tight in his hand.

"I said, cut it out."

But the Dwarf went on.

"How about three hundred thousand?"

Gil's voice rose as he spoke again.

"Cut it out or I'll hang up on you."

"You will?"

"You heard me."

"You never did that on me before."

"But I'll do it now."

"I believe you will."

"So cut it out."

"You're growing up, Gil. Growing up to be a man."

And he heard the Dwarf chuckle.

"Don't laugh at me."

"I'm not, Gil. I'm laughing with you this time."
"Okay."
"You have spirit. That's what I always liked about you, Gil. Spirit and guts and loyalty."
"You're putting me on again."
"No. I'm levelling with you. You have guts."
The Dwarf's voice had become low and serious.
"So?"
Gil was still angry at him.
"So I'm letting you know that. Just between brothers."
There was a slight pause.
Brothers, Gil thought.
It's been years since he used that word with me.
I can't remember when he last called me his brother.
And I haven't done it with him.
When did I last call him Brother?
When?
"Listen to me, Gil?"
In my horrible dreams.
That's when.
"Gil?"
"Well?"
"I've got to see you."
"Okay."
"But I can't get away from here."
Gil didn't speak.
"You still there?"
"Yes," Gil said.
"Then listen. You'll have to come in."
"To you?"
"To me."
"But why?"
"I'll tell you when I see you."
"Why can't you come up here?"
"No way."
"But . . ."
The Dwarf cut in on him.

"I just can't. You have to believe me."

"Let me think about it."

"There's no time for thinking. You've just got to do it."

"You mean to come in and then go back the same day?"

"Right. Just that and no more, Gil."

"Okay. I'll do it."

"That's the boy."

"Should I bring the ticket with me?"

"No."

"What?"

"Not yet."

"Don't you want it?"

"Sure I want it. But keep it buried for now."

"Why?"

"Just do what I say and save the questions."

"You'll answer them for me when I see you?"

"Every single one of them."

Gil was silent.

"Gil, there's six million dollars riding on you doing what I tell you to do. You got it now?"

No, Gil thought. I don't get it now.

And you put a chill in me, Dwarf.

But he heard himself say, almost wearily, "When do you want to see me?"

"Tomorrow."

"That's Saturday."

"I know it's Saturday."

"But I help out at the store. I can't get away."

"Find an excuse."

"I won't be able to."

"I said, find one."

"But, Dwarf, I . . . I . . ."

Gil's voice trailed off hopelessly. For he knew that he would have to do what the Dwarf wanted him to.

There was no way out.

He heard the Dwarf's harsh, commanding voice again.

"Be there at twelve or so. I'll be waiting for you."

"You still at the same place?"

"Yes. Dwarves always stay in the same places. We like our caves. It's pretty hard to find a good one these days. It was easier in past centuries."

Gil tried one more time.

"I don't know if I'll be able to get away."

"You will."

"Tomorrow is too short a notice."

"All life is a short notice. So be here."

"They really need me."

"I know that."

"They do."

"I know. But I need you more."

There was a sharp click.

And he knew that the Dwarf had hung up.

He sat there staring at the glowing branches and thinking.

I shouldn't go in.

And yet I know that I will.

8

"He called to say hello," Gil said. "That was all it was."

They had just finished with breakfast, he and his uncle. Aunt Edith had already gone on to the store.

"And?"

"Then I found out that he was sick and in bed."

His uncle took the cups that Gil had washed, held them up and examined them and then slowly, thoughtfully dried them.

"In bed?"

He set the cups into their places on the neat shelf and then turned back to Gil.

"Sorry to hear that."

"He's never that way. Never been sick as long as I know him."

"That's true. Gareth was always sturdy."

Gil handed him the last of the dishes.

"So I thought I'd just go in and see him for a few hours."

"What's wrong with him? Did he say?"

Gil shook his head.

"Only that he has some fever."

"Nobody's there with him?"

"You know how he lives."

"I know, Gil. Gareth's always been alone."

The man's gentle, wise eyes were quietly studying Gil. And Gil wondered if his uncle was seeing through the lies.

"I know how much you need me in the store."

"That's all right. We'll manage."

"Then I can go?"

"Yes. Stay overnight if you have to. Come back in the morning."

"You'll tell Aunt Edith?"

His uncle smiled at him.

"I'll take care of her, if that's what you mean."

"I'm sorry to do this. But he's my brother."

"He is, Gil."

The man patted him on the shoulder and then went to the hall closet and got his coat.

"I'll drive you in to the station if you want, Gil."

"I'd appreciate that."

"No trouble at all."

"Great."

"Train leaves every hour for New York. So you won't have much to wait."

"I'll be fine."

"Then let's do it."

When they opened the front door to go outside, the wind blew against them, bleak and harsh.

The door flew out of Gil's hands and slammed shut with an angry, fateful sound.

"Winter is coming on," his uncle said.

"It sure is."

"Be here before we even know it."

"Right."

They were now sitting in the car.

"Think it'll be a cold one, Gil?"

"I think so."

And Gil remembered the mailman asking him the same question.

The tall, lean mailman with the hard and piercing eyes,

the one who had brought him the winning ticket at sunset time.

He wondered where he was now.

You're a loner, he had said. It's a disease you never get rid of.

"You have enough money on you, Gil?"

"What?"

"Money? You have it?"

Gil nodded.

"Yes, Uncle Joe. Thanks."

"Watch your wallet in New York."

"I will."

"Where do you carry it?"

"My back pocket."

His uncle shook his head.

"You take it out and put it inside. Your inside pocket."

"But . . ."

"Just do it."

"Okay. If that's what you say."

"That's what I say."

Gil took out his wallet and then put it into the inside pocket of his leather windbreaker.

"That's more like it."

"I'm used to the other way, Uncle Joe."

The man shook his head firmly.

"The other way is no good these days, Gil. You got to be careful with money. That's all people think about these days. They kill each other for money, Gil. Just read your paper or listen to the six o'clock news. You know that."

"I do," Gil murmured.

A car passed by them and his uncle waved to the driver.

"I've seen money change people, Gil. Lots of money and just no money around. It did things to them. Went right inside of them and burnt them out. Burnt out their good and decent hearts. They became animals—real cruel animals.''

The two rode silently along the bleak, windswept road.

''Money creates a lot of problems.''

''It also solves them,'' Gil said.

His uncle turned to him with a quiet look.

''Never heard you talk that way.''

Gil shrugged.

''The thought just came to me, that's all.''

''Never heard you talk that way,'' his uncle said again.

And then Gil said to himself, neither did I.

Am I changing?

Is it because of the money the ticket stands for that I've lied so much to my uncle and aunt?

Is the money changing me?

Three million dollars has a lot of power to it.

It can do an awful lot of things.

And yet how much will the Dwarf give me?

Maybe not even a red cent.

And yet the thought of all that money holds me tight, like in a vise.

''Here we are, Gil.''

Gil got out of the car and felt the force of the wind upon him.

''I'll be back tonight,'' he said.

''All right. But take care of yourself.''

''I will, Uncle Joe.''

''And tell Gareth to feel better.''

''I'll be sure to.''

''Just take care.''

Gil stood silently and watched the dark car go slowly off and then turn a windy corner and vanish from his view.

He suddenly felt alone and lost.

As if his uncle had gone off and deserted him.

Never to see him again.

Just like his father had done.

9

It was on the train to New York that it happened.

Just after the Chatham stop.

Just then.

Gil was sitting looking through the window at the gray sky and the waving branches of the bare trees, when he felt somebody heavy ease into the seat next to him.

Gil kept looking through the window.

The train picked up speed.

"Hello."

Gil turned and saw the man sitting next to him.

"Mind if I sit here?"

"Not at all," Gil said.

The man had a rugged, almost battered face. He must've been a fighter, Gil thought, and fought too many hard fights.

He was big and he had on a dark blue coat and a gray felt hat. The brim was over the eyes.

"Some people mind when you sit down next to them. I can feel it and I don't like it. You're not one of those people, are you?"

It was a low, easy voice. It did not go with the face.

"No," Gil said.

A diamond ring sparkled on one of the man's thick,

knobby fingers. Gil looked up to the broad face with the harsh planes to it.

The eyes were brown and veiled.

They could become cruel eyes, Gil thought.

"Then I feel good."

The man opened a *New York Times* and began to read it.

Gil turned back to the window.

The train was passing a row of small new houses, all alike. A man was getting into his car, a woman was standing in the doorway with a small child at her side, and they both were waving at him. Suddenly Gil heard the man speak again.

Quietly.

So very quietly.

"You're the Dwarf's brother, aren't you?"

Gil felt the blood run cold within him.

He didn't answer.

The man chuckled.

"Sure you are."

Gil turned and looked into the brown eyes.

They were cold and bright.

So very bright.

"I'm Milo. One of the Dwarf's friends."

"Friends?"

Yet the chill did not leave him.

"Sure. The Dwarf and I go to the fights and the races together. He's a great sports fan. Did you know that, Gil?"

"No."

Milo leaned back and smiled.

"Lots of things you don't know about the Dwarf. But you'll learn."

Gil didn't speak.

"He likes to make a bet every now and then. Sometimes he wins and sometimes he loses. You're going in to see him, aren't you?"

"Yes."

Milo laughed, a soft easy laugh.

"I was right."

"You were," Gil said.

"Going in to see the Dwarf."

Milo turned back to his newspaper. Gil no longer looked out the window. He just stared straight ahead of him.

"I like to read the *Times.* It's a good paper. Makes me feel like an intellectual. That's what it does."

Gil turned back to the battered face.

The eyes now had a mocking look in them.

The voice was quiet.

So very quiet.

"You ever read it, Gil?"

"Yes."

"You get it up your way?"

"Yes."

"Every day? Or only on Sundays?"

"Every day."

"How much does it cost up your way?"

"Forty cents."

"Cost me thirty cents. So I got you beat."

"Guess you have."

Milo looked squarely at Gil and with his large hands delicately began to fold up his newspaper.

"Got you beat, Gil," he said softly. "Remember that."

Gil was silent.

"You and the Dwarf."

The train began to slow down and Milo rose to his feet.

"I get off here," he said.

Gil looked up at him and didn't say anything.

"I'm going to give you a message for the Dwarf."

The man suddenly leaned over to Gil, his eyes narrowing.

"Tell him Gordie is getting tired of words. You got that?"

Gil slowly nodded.

"The words will end. The action will begin. You got that?"

"Yes."

"Soon. Very soon."

Then Milo turned and went down the aisle and out of the train.

10

It had begun to rain.

A chilling, autumn rain.

He walked down the deserted street till he came to number 32. That was one of the numbers the Dwarf had played, he thought to himself.

One of the lucky numbers.

Gil stopped and looked up at the old gray loft building that had been converted from a clothing factory into apartments, some years ago.

The Dwarf lived on the top floor of the building.

Fifth floor back.

Gil stared at the gloomy facade, the old fire escapes, wet and dripping in the slanting rain. A truck sped by and Gil turned and watched it, listening to the swishing of the huge tires on the wet cobblestones of the old street. Then he turned and went inside the building and into the old elevator.

The dingy freight elevator stalled on the fourth floor. Gil had to get out there, then go up a flight of creaky wooden stairs to the floor above.

No one had been on the elevator with him.

No one was now in the corridor that was lit by a single overhead bulb. The light from the bulb was weak and its rays faded on the dark blue walls.

Gil stopped at the end of the silent corridor and knocked on the door.

There was no answer.

He knocked again.

Then he heard a voice from inside, close to the door.

"Who is it?"

It was the Dwarf's harsh voice.

"Gil."

"You alone?"

"Yes."

"Wait."

He heard the sound of a chair being brought to the door. Then he heard the Dwarf get onto the chair.

"Stand back, Gil."

He saw an eye stare out at him through the tiny peephole in the door.

"Move away from the door, Gil."

"Why?"

Gil's nerves were on edge.

"You do as I say."

Gil moved back into the silent, shadowy corridor.

Then he heard the Dwarf's voice again.

"All right. You're alone."

"I told you I was."

Gil wanted to get out of the corridor and inside behind the protecting door. He kept feeling that there was someone on the staircase, standing on the top step, coldly watching him.

He turned suddenly, but there was nobody there.

Only the shadowy darkness.

"What's holding you up?"

"Keep your shirt on, Gil."

He heard the scrape of the chair as it was being pushed aside and then the door opened on a chain and the Dwarf peered through the slight opening and up at Gil, and then the chain was taken off and Gil went inside.

The Dwarf shut the door and then locked it.

"I just had to make sure," he said.

"Why?"

The Dwarf didn't answer.

Gil noted that the locks were set low, within reach of the Dwarf. There were three of them.

He used to have only one, he thought to himself.

Did the change come before or after the winning ticket?

"You eat yet?"

"No," he said.

Gil kept looking down at his brother. At the dark, curly hair, the large features and the deep black eyes.

At the grotesquely small body that was under the large face.

I don't know if I ever got used to it, he thought.

"You hungry?"

"Yes."

Does one ever get used to it?

Ever?

"I got lunch set up for you."

"Thanks."

Even my mother didn't. I know that. I know that in my heart of hearts. No, she tried and tried.

But she never did.

In the end it broke her heart.

And my father?

He just walked away from it.

"I'll heat it up, Gil."

"Want any help?"

"It's all ready."

Gil watched the Dwarf go off on his little legs to the kitchen and then he stood and gazed about him. His eyes paused on the chairs that were scaled down to fit his brother.

The small couch.

The low bed.

Then some chairs that were normal size.

Normal, he said to himself and a great sadness went into him.

"You want some coffee?" the Dwarf called out from the kitchen.

"Okay."

"You take Sanka or the real stuff?"

"Regular, Dwarf."

"You got it."

The room Gil was standing in was large and low-ceilinged. Three of the walls were bare. But on the fourth wall was a huge reproduction of Las Meninas. Gil walked over to it and lit a lamp and then stood enjoying the great painting that Velasquez had created centuries ago.

The glowing figures.

The artist himself at his easel, the princess and her dwarf attendant.

"Mari Barbella," Gil murmured.

The little dwarf looked right out at you, her deep brown eyes large and gentle.

Gil knew why his brother loved the painting.

And cared for no other.

"What are you waiting for?"

The Dwarf was on the threshold, his shadow grotesque on the wooden floor.

"Just looking at things."

His brother came over to him on his short, quick legs.

"Mari Barbella?"

"Yes," Gil said.

There was a clean light in his brother's eyes.

"She's lovely, isn't she?"

Clean and bright.

She wasn't really, and yet Gil could see that she was. Yes, once you looked at her through his brother's eyes.

Now she was very lovely, he thought.

And so gentle and soft against his bitter harshness.

I should try to see the world the way he sees it.

I should really try.

Nobody else ever does.

Then he heard the Dwarf's voice and it was strangely low and appealing.

"She lived centuries ago, Gil. If I had been born then I would have been a very esteemed member of King Phillip's court and been married to Mari Barbella. Ever think of that, Gil?"

"No," Gil said gently.

The rain ran against the windows.

His brother began to speak again.

"And then again who knows if she would've wanted me?"

"She would have," Gil said.

"You think so?"

"Yes, Dwarf."

They stood there looking at the light and shadow play over the painting.

"I would've had everything I wanted," his brother said. "The finest of clothes. The best of foods. Everything my heart desired. I was born four centuries too late. Or was it three?"

"I think it was four," Gil said.

He found out later that he was wrong and that his brother was right. But by that time it was too late to tell him.

"You sure it's four?"

"Yes."

"There you see. I even got that wrong."

The Dwarf turned abruptly and went back into the kitchen. Gil stood there awhile still looking at the painting.

Mari Barbella and the Dwarf.

Yes.

They would've been happy.

I would bet my life on it.

"Come in and keep me company."

Gil turned away from the painting.

"Okay."

He went into the kitchen and slowly sat down on one

of the normal-sized chairs. His brother was at the gas range, stirring the spaghetti.

He stood on a low bench.

Gil sat there, watching him.

"Apartment looks good," he said.

The Dwarf waved his small hand.

"It's all the same. All the same. I never change anything."

"Looks different."

"The same."

"Haven't been here in a long while."

"So you're here now."

"Yes," Gil said. "I'm here now."

The Dwarf came over to the table and reached up and set a plate of hot steaming spaghetti on it.

"It's Ronzoni. The brand you like."

"You remembered that?"

"Uh-huh."

Gil smiled down at him.

"I still like it."

"Then eat."

"How about you?"

The Dwarf shook his head.

"I've had mine already."

Gil began to eat and his brother stood against the stove, barely topping it, and watched him.

There was a gentle look in his eyes.

"Tastes real good."

"There's more in the pot. All for you."

"Okay with me."

"You've got a bit taller, didn't you?"

Gil paused.

"About an inch or so."

"Your hair looks blonder. You bleach it?"

Gil laughed.

"No, Dwarf."

"Some kids bleach their hair now."

"Not me."

"I see them walking around Greenwich Village."
"They're weirdos."
"And you're not one of them?"
"You know I'm not."
"I do."
The Dwarf smiled one of his rare smiles and Gil saw how quiet his eyes could become, quiet and at rest, and how serene his face could be.
No more at war with the world.
Or the world with him.
"You're a handsome guy, Gil. The girls let you alone?"
"Cut it out, Dwarf," Gil said.
"You have a favorite? She pretty?"
"The spaghetti is very good. You cook up a storm."
The Dwarf smiled again.
"Okay. I'll let you alone."
Then they were silent and the rain swept against the window and Gil found himself thinking about Milo.
Sitting on the train again and hearing the man's hard voice.
He paused in his eating and then slowly let the fork settle back onto the plate again.
"What's the matter, Gil?"
"Nothing."
Gil tried to eat again, but he couldn't.
"What is it?"
Gil turned and looked at the Dwarf.
"I met a fellow on the train."
"And?"
"He said he was a friend of yours."
"I have no friends on trains."
"He said he was."
"Go on."
"He said his name was Milo."
"What?"
The Dwarf came closer to Gil.
"A big guy. Looked like a fighter."

"Milo was a fighter," the Dwarf said.

His face had tightened, his eyes had become dark and hard, and his little strong hands were clenched into fists.

"Milo," he almost whispered the name.

"He got on the train at Chatham."

"And?"

"And then he sat down next to me."

"Just like that?"

"Like he knew me."

"Finish your coffee and do the dishes," the Dwarf suddenly said.

His voice was harsh and cold.

"But . . ."

"Do it."

Then he turned away from Gil and went out of the kitchen, not saying another word to him.

Gil sat there, not eating anymore, the coffee in the cup becoming cold, and then he slowly rose and put the dishes into the sink and washed them and put them into the drying rack, one after the other, and all the time he knew that the Dwarf was in the other room.

Alone and silent.

Finally, he went inside to him.

The Dwarf was sitting in one of his chairs, staring at the wooden floor. He didn't even look up when Gil came into the room.

"A big guy. With a pushed-in face."

"Yes," Gil said.

"How did he know you were on the train?"

Gil shook his head.

"No idea."

The rain had slackened, but the sky was still dark, and the shadows lay in the corners of the room.

"Who told him who you were?"

Gil didn't answer.

"Who could've told him?"

The Dwarf seemed to be speaking to himself.

Gil could barely hear him.

"That's what I'd like to know."

"Someone told him."

Gil went over to his brother.

"Dwarf, what is this all about?"

"Nothing."

"What do you mean nothing?"

"Just what I said."

"He had a message for you," Gil said.

Now his brother looked up at him.

"What was it?"

"He said, 'Gordie is getting tired of words.' "

"So?"

"The action will soon begin."

"The action, eh."

"Yes."

The Dwarf's thick lips tightened.

"Then let it."

"Dwarf."

"I'll be able to handle it."

He turned silently away from Gil.

"Handle what?" Gil asked.

But there was no answer.

"What does he mean by action? What?"

The Dwarf got up and went to the window and stood there looking out at the bleak rain.

"Gordie was my friend. My best friend," he said bitterly. "All through the years. And now look at him."

Gil went over to the window and stood by his brother.

"Dwarf, what's going on?"

"Nothing."

"You've got to tell me."

"Just stay out of this, Gil."

"What do you mean stay out of it? You made me a part of it."

The Dwarf looked up at him.

"No, Gil."

"Can't you see it?"

"I tell you, no."

Gil's voice rose as he spoke again.

"I am in it."

The Dwarf looked up at him and Gil never forgot that stricken look. Long after it was all over he could still see those deep black eyes.

With such sorrow in them.

"I never meant to, Gil," he said.

"Whether you meant to or not, I'm in it. I can feel it in my bones. And I don't like the feeling at all, Dwarf. I don't."

His brother looked away from him and didn't speak.

"You've got to tell me."

"The money," the Dwarf said without turning. "What else could it be about?"

The money, Gil thought.

Always the money.

"Gordie wants it all."

"All?"

"He wants me to give up my half of the ticket. He'll go in and cash it and then throw me a hundred thousand or so."

"I don't get it."

"I don't either. We were partners for years in the tickets. We started it one day. We were both a bit drunk and we bought a ticket and then tore it in half and he took one half and I took the other. It was a day number ticket. And we won a grand that time and we split it. And that's how it's been down through the years. And now . . . And now he . . . he wants it all."

His voice faded away into silence.

Only the sound of the rain on the window remained.

Only that.

"You were partners," Gil said. "You're still partners. Half of that money is yours. Three million of it."

"We're partners. But I'm a Dwarf."

Gil stared down at him.

"What do you mean by that?"

"Just what I said. Gordie figures why should a Dwarf

get all that money? He's only a Dwarf. A half-person. A nothing man. So why give him anything? Why? The lion gets it all. Isn't that the way it is every time? Aesop saw it way back. Remember the Lion and the . . . So he throws me a bone."

"I don't believe this," Gil said.

His brother turned sharply to him.

"Live a little longer, Gil. Hope a little longer. And then you'll see your hopes smashed. And you'll believe anything and everything in this stinking world of yours."

Gil was silent.

"Anything," the Dwarf said bitterly.

"So he wants the ticket."

"That's about it."

"And he thinks you have it here?"

"Yes."

"Did he know that you were sending the tickets to me?"

The Dwarf shook his head.

"I never told anybody that."

"And that's why you had me bury the winning ticket?"

"Just to make sure it was safe until I needed it."

They were both silent again.

"But the ticket is worthless unless the two of you get together."

The Dwarf nodded.

"I know. And Gordie knows."

"Then you . . . ?"

"I'm waiting for Gordie to come around and stop all this."

"If he doesn't?"

"He will when he sees he can't budge me."

"He's talking about action."

The Dwarf waved his little hand with contempt. His black eyes flashed.

"Let him talk. He'll get nowhere."

And Gil remembered what his uncle had said about money and people.

They kill each other for money.

He had said it with the wind blowing around them, the cold autumn wind.

Six million dollars is an awful lot of money, Gil thought.

A killing lot.

"Milo looks to be a man who will do anything for a buck," Gil said.

"He is that kind."

"A big, cruel man. That's the way I size him up."

The Dwarf nodded.

"He's hurt people before. Maybe even killed one or two. Or three."

Gil looked at him.

"What?"

The Dwarf shook his head slowly.

"It's not Milo. It's Gordie. He's the worse of the two. I can see that now, Gil. Only now."

His voice was quiet and low and yet Gil could see a trace of anxiety and fear in the dark eyes.

"You should go to the police."

"The police? Don't make me laugh."

"You should."

The Dwarf shook his head grimly.

"No. It's between Gordie and me. That's the way it is, Gil."

"How is it going to end?"

"The way I say it will."

Gil gazed through the window at the wet, blind walls of the building opposite them.

The rain dripping down the old gray bricks, dripping endlessly.

Like trickles of blood.

He felt blocked in and hopeless.

How was it really going to end? he asked himself.

"Dwarf," he said.

"Well?"
"Why did you want to see me?"
"What do you mean?"
"It's more than a year since the last time. Why now?"
The Dwarf didn't answer.
"You said, don't bring the ticket. So why did you want to see me? You've been using the telephone all the time."
Still his brother didn't answer him.
"Why?"
"Just felt like it."
"It's been such a long time."
"I told you I felt like seeing you. Don't push me."
The Dwarf's voice had become harsh again.
"It's something else," Gil said.
They stood looking at each other.
Their shadows were silent and still on the bare wall.
"Maybe it is, Gil."
Gil waited.
"I'll tell you when it's all over," the Dwarf said.
"No."
"That's how it's going to be."
"I want to know now."
The Dwarf slowly and grimly shook his head.
"No use pushing me. That's how I'm made up. Nobody pushes me."
"Please tell me."
"When it's all over. And I have my three million. Only then, Gil."
And Gil knew it was futile to ask anymore.
They stood by the rain-streaked window, the two brothers, their shadows falling harshly on the flat wall.
One shadow was tall and straight, and the other, a black shadow, short and grotesque.
Gil glanced over to the wall and he found himself thinking of the handsome prince and the ugly frog.
For an instant he seemed to be thrust back into the terrifying dream.

A chill went through him to the core of his being.

He trembled.

And then he heard the Dwarf's voice.

"Go back home, Gil. And wait till you hear from me again."

Gil struggled back and out of the dream.

"What?"

His brother was looking sharply at him.

"What's wrong?"

"Nothing."

"You got awfully white."

"I'm okay."

"You shivered."

"I said I'm okay."

"You sure?"

"Yes, I tell you. Leave me alone."

Within him, deep within him, he felt a rush of fear and shame. And he thought to himself, if my brother only knew of the dream . . .

Of how terrified I am of being turned into a dwarf like him.

Terrified and ashamed.

If he knew!

How could I ever face him again?

"Gil."

But I can't help having the dream.

I just can't.

It comes in and there's nothing I can do about it.

It's a curse. A curse.

"Gil."

The Dwarf kept looking at him and Gil wondered if he had penetrated into the secret of the dream.

But when he spoke his voice was calm and his face impassive.

"Go home. Nobody's going to bother you. It's me they're after."

Gil just stood there and was silent.

"You'll be all right, I tell you. There is nothing they want from you."

Gil took a deep breath.

"I'm not thinking of myself," he said.

"What do you mean?"

"I don't like leaving you this way."

The Dwarf smiled at him.

"I'm the big brother. Not you."

Gil looked down at him.

"You are," he said gently.

"I'm small. But I'm tough. Hard to beat."

Gil didn't say anything.

"Get that sad look off your face."

"All right."

"I'll be just fine. No sweat."

"You'll take care of yourself?"

"Sure."

He put his hand out to Gil and Gil held it and then let it go.

"I'm your big brother. Always remember that."

Gil never forgot those words as long as he lived.

11

He turned down a rainy side street on his way to the subway station when a cab pulled up at the curb.

The driver leaned out of the window and motioned to him.

"Hey, buddy."

Gil went over to him.

"Where's Houston Street?"

"The next block over," Gil said and was about to turn away.

"Come in and show us," a voice called from the back of the cab.

Gil swung around and saw the man.

It was Milo.

"What do you want?"

The door of the cab opened.

"Get in," Milo said. "Take a ride with me."

Gil looked wildly about him at the deserted rainy street with its silent old buildings.

He turned to run when he heard Milo's sharp voice.

"Don't try it."

And then he saw the gun in Milo's big hand.

"Get in and don't give me any trouble. Move fast."

"Leave me alone."

"Get in."

Gil silently went into the cab and sat down. The door slammed shut and the cab pulled swiftly away from the curb.

It headed west, towards the river.

"What do you want with me?"

"Nothing. Just like having you at my side."

Gil felt the cold barrel of the gun, hard against him.

"Let me go home," he said.

"In time. After you've seen Gordie."

"What does he want?"

"Ask him yourself."

The cab drove along the cobbled streets and the only sound Gil heard was that of rhythmic window wipers.

Again and again and again.

Like the relentless strokes of fate.

I'm caught, he said to himself. I'm caught in something that has me tight as a vise.

I can see that now.

Why did the Dwarf get me into this?

Why?

They stopped for a red light and a police car pulled up alongside of them and the policeman lowered his window and looked across at them.

Gil gazed desperately at him.

"Speak and you're dead," Milo whispered.

"Your taillights are out," the policeman said to the driver.

"Sorry. Didn't know it."

"Get them fixed."

"Sure will, Officer."

The policeman kept looking at Gil. Gil opened his lips and then hopelessly shut them.

"Don't move," Milo murmured.

The light changed and the police car drove off ahead of them. Gil watched the car disappear in the rain.

"I see you're going to be a good boy," Milo said.

"Nobody likes to die young," the driver said.

"Nobody likes to die anytime," Milo said.

Both men laughed.

And listening to that harsh laughter Gil knew that Milo would surely have killed him if he had tried to call out to the policeman.

Then he would have turned the gun on the cop and killed him, too.

These are lost people, he said to himself.

Forever lost.

Because they have nothing more to lose.

The cab turned down the next block and then went slowly up the street till it stopped in front of an old loft building.

Just like the Dwarf's, Gil thought.

They waited for a lone man to pass by them and disappear around the empty rainswept corner.

"All right," Milo said.

He reached over and opened the door.

"Now we're going in here and you keep your mouth shut if we meet anybody on the way up. You got it?"

Gil didn't answer him.

"Speak up."

"Yes," Gil said.

"Good."

"Should I wait here?" the driver asked.

"It all depends on what happens upstairs."

"I'll wait, Milo. Till you come down and tell me."

"Okay."

He turned to Gil and shoved him.

"Get out. And remember what I said. Don't give me any trouble or it'll be the last you'll ever give anybody. Get it?"

Gil didn't speak.

"Well?"

Gil nodded.

"Cat got your tongue?"

Milo pushed him forward through the rain and into the doorway of the old bleak building.

"Get into the elevator."

They stood close to each other as the elevator rose wearily to the third floor. Gil could feel the man's cold breath on the nape of his neck.

He clenched his hands to keep them from trembling.

He thought again of the Dwarf and was bitter.

Go on home, he said.

They want nothing from you.

It's me they're after.

Go on home.

Will I ever see home again?

They got out of the elevator and Milo pointed without a word to a door that was at the end of the carpeted corridor.

The carpet was gray and faded.

They stopped at a door that had a brass-rimmed peephole. The brass glinted under the overhead light.

All was still about them.

Milo put his thick finger to the bell button and pressed it three times.

He did it again.

The door was finally opened by a woman.

"Come in."

"I got him, Casey," Milo said.

She closed the door behind her, locked it, and then looked quietly at Gil. Her eyes studied him.

"You're scared, aren't you?"

Gil didn't answer.

Her hand touched him gently on his cheek.

"Well, don't be. You'll be all right."

He still felt her soft hand long after it was gone from him.

Soft and soothing.

"Sure he will." Milo laughed harshly.

The woman turned coldly to him.

"Lay off that stuff."

"I'm only trying to . . ."

"Just leave it alone," she said.

"Sure thing, Casey."

"It looks like you roughed him up. You were told not to."

"I didn't touch him."

"None of your jungle stuff. Gordie promised me that."

Milo shook his head and an anxious and almost timid look came onto the battered face.

"I didn't, Casey. I tell you I didn't."

She turned away from him and they walked down a narrow hall and then into a living room. It was large and high, but the walls and the furniture were old and worn. The drapes hanging over the long wet windows were gray and dusty.

A man put down his glass on an end table and got up from one of the couches and slowly came over to them.

"So he's here."

"He is."

"Okay, Milo. You wait in the other room."

"Whatever you say, Gordie."

"I'll call you if I need you."

"You won't need him," the woman said. "Send him away."

The man turned quietly to her.

"You leave that to me, Case."

"I said you won't need him. This is a kid."

"It's a kid who can get us the money."

"I don't want any rough stuff, Gordie. You promised me that."

"There won't be."

"I said I don't want it. Put the gorilla back in his cage."

"Go in the other room, Milo."

"Gordie," the woman said.

"Go on, Milo. And wait there."

Milo silently left them.

"You're going downhill, Gordie. Ever since the ticket."

"I've been going downhill all my life, Case. Just like you."

The man turned abruptly away from her and then motioned Gil to a chair.

"Sit down. Nobody's going to hurt you."

Gil did not move.

He kept looking to the woman. His eyes appealed desperately to her. And then their eyes met and he felt a little of his chilling fear leave him.

Just a little.

But it was enough to help him keep his balance and not give way to complete terror.

The woman.

She was of medium height, slightly built, with reddish-brown hair, large blue eyes and small, fine features.

He kept watching her.

She must've been close to forty, but there was a faded, worn look to her that made her seem older to him. It was the eyes that did that, he thought. For deep in them, deep in their soft blue he could sense an ever-present dark sadness.

A sadness and a despair.

"Let him unwind, Gordie," she said.

He slowly nodded.

"All right, Case."

He was still a good-looking man. Tall and lean with a sharp-featured face. He had high cheekbones and thin, well-shaped lips. His hands were long and the fingers expressive and strong. His eyes were brown.

Somber and reflective eyes.

The voice was low and controlled.

Gil wondered what lay behind it—what inner cruelty.

"Sit down."

Gil walked over to one of the chairs, his legs still feeling shaky. He slowly sat down.

"Do you want a drink? A beer? Ginger ale?"

"No," Gil said.

"You look thirsty."

"Nothing."

"Just name it."

"He said no, Gordie."

"So he did."

A thin mocking smile had come to his lips.

"I've been drinking Scotch and soda. Why don't you try one? Your name is Gil, isn't it?"

"Gordie."

He glanced over to her.

"Just trying to be sociable."

"You're not. Let him relax."

"That's what I'm trying to do."

"You're needling him. And liking it."

"Was I?"

"Yes. You were."

He laughed softly.

"Didn't realize it. Didn't realize it at all, Case."

"Now you're trying to needle me."

"Am I?"

"Yes."

The lamplight fell across her taut face.

"How am I doing?"

"Better than you think."

"Then I'll keep it up."

"You'd better not."

He laughed again and Gil, watching them, felt a cold hatred for the man.

A hatred and a fear.

He remembered the Dwarf's words and the Dwarf's somber face as he said them: Gordie is worse than Milo.

Much worse.

"I'll be nice," Gordie said.

He went back to his sofa and sat down. Then he picked up his glass and stirred his drink.

Slowly, methodically.

The rain became strong again and lashed against the windows.

Gil listened desperately.

The sound of the fierce rain fighting to break through the glass wall of the windows and reach into the room seemed to give him strength.

To settle Gil down.

Gordie began to speak to him.

"You're wondering why we got you here."

"Yes," Gil said.

"What do you think?"

"I don't know."

"But of course you do. It's a matter of six million dollars. A very small matter, don't you think?"

Gil looked over to him.

"But what have I to do with all this?"

"Everything."

"I don't get it."

"You're the Dwarf's brother, aren't you?"

"So?"

"His only brother. There's nobody else, is there?"

"Nobody else," Gil said.

"Your aunt and uncle don't mean anything to him."

Gil was silent.

"He used to curse them. Especially your aunt."

"He never did," Gil said, his eyes flashing.

Gordie set down his glass.

"I know the Dwarf better than you ever will. Brother or not. We used to be the best of friends. For years. Till the money came along."

Till the money came along, Gil thought bitterly.

"He told me they threw him out of the house."

"That's a lie," Gil said.

"Is it?"

"Nobody ever threw him out. He left of his own will. Just left and came here."

"Let it alone," Case said.

Gordie looked over to her and then back to Gil.

"With the Dwarf you never know the truth," he said quietly.

And for an instant the dark thought came to Gil: With the Dwarf you never know. You never really know.

He wears too many masks.

You rarely see the true face beneath the mask.

You never know.

The rain lashed the windows again and Gil drove the thoughts away from him.

Gordie was speaking again.

"But this thing I'm sure of," he said. "That you're the only person in this world the Dwarf has any feelings for. He hates everybody but you. I know it."

Gil didn't speak.

"Why did you come in to see him?"

"Because he asked me to."

Gordie shook his head.

"He never has visitors. He lives alone, a man in his cave."

"I told you he wanted to see me. I'm his brother."

"He wanted to see you and tell you where he's hidden his part of the ticket. That's why."

"I don't know anything about a ticket."

Gordie's hand tightened about his glass.

"You called me a liar. And now I'm calling you one," he said harshly.

"Take it easy, Gordie," Case said.

"You take it easy."

He got up from the couch and came over to Gil.

"You know everything about the ticket. Why did he call you in?"

"Just to see me. He hasn't seen me in a year. It was time."

Gordie's lips thinned into a hard line.

"He showed you where he's hidden the ticket. So if anything's happened to him then you'll get hold of it. Isn't that it?"

Gil shook his head.

"I don't know what you're talking about."

"He's coming to the end of the stick. And he knows it."

Gil looked up into the dark eyes.

"You're going to kill him, aren't you?"

"If he doesn't come up with that ticket."

Gil turned desperately to Casey and he saw that her face was taut and pale.

"Why do you want all the money?" he suddenly cried out to her. "When half should go to the Dwarf?"

She didn't answer him.

"Is that what he told you?" Gordie asked.

Gil turned back to him.

"It's the truth, isn't it?"

Gordie shook his head grimly.

"It's just the other way around. It's the Dwarf who wants it all."

"I don't believe you."

"Because he's conned you."

"He hasn't."

"Listen to me. Listen, you young fool."

"I tell you he . . ."

But Gordie cut in on him.

"Listen. I was ready to go down with him the day we hit. Down to the lottery office with my half of the ticket and he with his. The both of us. He agreed to be there."

"And?"

"He never showed up. Never."

Gil looked away from his tense figure to Casey.

But her tight, pale face told him nothing.

"He wants it all. He'll throw us a bone. That's how it is. He says he'll destroy his ticket if he doesn't get his way. Nobody will get anything."

"No," Gil said.

"Yes. Yes. That's how it is. He's a Dwarf. When the chips are down he's a Dwarf. An evil Dwarf."

Gil remembered what his aunt had said.

She had used those exact words.

He's an evil Dwarf, Gil.

"He belongs back in the Dark Ages. He never left them. With his ugly face, his little body and his black heart."

"I still don't believe you," Gil said.

"You don't?"

"No."

Gordie suddenly hit Gil hard across the mouth with the flat of his hand. Gil staggered back.

"I don't care whether you believe me or not. I want that ticket."

"I don't know where it is," Gil said and he felt a trickle of blood coming from his lip.

"Gordie."

Casey came swiftly over to them.

"Stay out of this."

"Let him alone," she said.

"I don't know where it is," Gil said again.

"You do. I know you do."

He raised his hand again and she put herself between them. And for an instant Gil felt that Gordie was going to hit her, too.

"Why don't you believe him, Gordie?"

"Because he's lying to me."

"I believe him."

"I don't."

He turned fiercely to Gil.

"I'm giving you your last chance. The words are over."

Gil looked away from him and over to Casey.

His eyes pleaded with her.

"Use your head," Gordie said in a low and hard voice. "When six million dollars is pushing a man he'll do anything to get it. Anything. Even if he's a saint. And I'm no saint. Ask her."

"Gordie," Casey said. "Please. You promised me."

But he didn't even turn to her.

"Do you want the truth beaten out of you?"

"I'm telling you the truth."

"Answer me."

Gil took his hand away from his swollen lip and saw the drops of blood on his fingertips and said nothing.

He heard Gordie speak again.

"All right. If that's the way you want it."

"Gordie, no. Keep Milo out of this."

"Shut up."

Then Gil saw the man push Casey away from him, turn and go out of the room.

And now all he could hear was the sound of the rain against the windows. And all he could feel was the great and chilling fear that was slowly spreading within him.

Making him tremble.

"He's gone for Milo," Casey said.

"Why don't they leave me alone?"

She came over close to him.

"He told you why."

"The money."

Her hand touched his face tenderly.

"Gil, do you know where the ticket is?"

He didn't answer her.

"Could you trust me?"

He still didn't answer her.

"I'm on your side. Believe me."

Are you? he asked himself bewilderedly.

Are you?

"Where is the ticket? I know the Dwarf has told you. I've good reason to know that."

He looked away from her and down to his hand.

"Trust me, Gil."

"Why should I?" he asked sullenly.

"Because I want to see the Dwarf get what is his and Gordie what belongs to him. It's not going to happen this way."

"But what can you do about it?"

"You've got to trust me."

He kept looking at her, trying to probe the truth.

"Gil, you've got to. It's the only way to save yourself and the Dwarf."

There were tears in her eyes.

"I know what's going on inside of you. I know it too well. But look at me and then follow your feelings about me. Just do it that way. Don't think. Just let your feelings make your decision for you. That way, Gil."

And if I tell you, he said to himself. If I tell you and you double cross me, then where am I?

And the Dwarf?

Where is he?

"Gil, take the chance."

And yet I've got nowhere to go but with her.

"Tell me before they come back."

Nowhere.

"Gil, before it's too late."

And then he saw that it was too late. For Gordie had come back into the room and Milo was close behind him.

"I gave you enough time to think it over," Gordie said.

Casey turned to him.

"Give him a little more time, Gordie. Just a little more."

He shook his head grimly.

"Well? Where is the ticket?"

Gil felt his heart begin to pound within him and his hands to shake.

"Well? Speak up."

"I don't know," Gil said.

Gordie's face whitened and then he motioned to Milo.

"He's all yours."

"Gordie, no," Casey cried out.

He pushed her away from him and she fell onto the couch.

"Leave no bruises or marks," he said quietly to Milo. "Don't touch his face."

"Okay."

Gil clenched his hands and stood rigid as Milo slowly approached him.

"The ticket," Milo said.

Gil pressed his lips together.

"The ticket."

Milo was now on him.

"The ticket."

He raised his hand and there was a short rubber hose tight in his massive fist.

"The ticket."

It belongs to the Dwarf, Gil said to himself. I must always remember that. No matter what happens to me.

No matter how great the pain.

No matter how scared I get.

It belongs to the Dwarf.

To my brother, the Dwarf.

12

He opened his eyes to a dark silence.

Then he heard her voice.

"Gil?"

He could see her face, pale and shadowy near him. Then he could make out the dim outlines of a chair.

And beyond that the dark wall.

Suddenly the lamp went on.

And he saw that she was sitting in a chair close to him. And he was lying on a bed, still in his clothes, and that outside the night had come down.

The rain had stopped.

Now all he could hear was the desolate sound of the autumn wind against the window. He thought of home, of his aunt and his uncle.

And of the Dwarf.

"How do you feel?"

"Weak."

"I've been taking care of you."

"Where are they?"

"Gone. For a while."

He tried to move and felt an aching pain in his ribs. He gasped out. She got up and leaned over him.

"Nothing is broken, Gil. Just try to lie back again."

He put his hand fearfully to his face, over his eyes and his nose and then his lips.

Milo had left his face alone.

"I started screaming," she said in a low voice. "Until they had to stop."

"Where are they?"

"Out looking for the Dwarf."

He lay on the bed and stared hopelessly at the wall.

"They'll be back," she said.

He just lay there listening to the wind.

"But I'm getting you out of here before that."

He looked away from the white shadowy wall and over to her.

"Yes, Gil. Nobody's going to hurt you again."

"The Dwarf?"

"They couldn't find him. He's gone into hiding. And that's what I'm going to do with you."

"What do you mean?"

"I'm taking you out of here before they come back."

"Where?"

"I have a place. Rest a bit more and then we'll go."

She was silent and then he saw her get up and go into a shadowy corner of the room and bend her head and he knew that she was crying.

Silently.

Deeply.

He shut his eyes and it seemed only a minute later that he heard her voice close to him.

"Gil?"

He felt her hand touching his hair.

"Yes?"

"We have to go."

"Oh."

"Our time is running out. Do you think you can get up?"

"Maybe."

"Try."

He tried and then fell back onto the bed again.

"Once more," she said gently. "You've got to do it. I know how much it hurts. But you've got to do it."

"All right," he murmured.

She sat on the bed by him and then put her arm behind his back and then helped him to sit up.

His ribs felt like they were on fire.

The sweat broke out onto his forehead.

"Now try to stand up."

He put one foot down onto the floor and then with her help put the other foot slowly down.

He pressed his lips tightly together and rose up.

He felt a scream of pain welling to his lips, but he fought it back.

He let out a loud gasp.

Loud and agonized.

"Put your arm around me."

He walked step by step with her out of the bedroom and then she let him sit down for a moment in the living room while she got his jacket.

She came over to him and draped it over his shoulders.

"You have to stand up again, Gil."

He went through the agony of rising up again, and all the time her large eyes were tenderly and anxiously upon him.

Are you on my side? he thought.

Are you?

"Now we have to make it to the door."

Or are you still with them?

Playing a savage, devilish game with me.

"Yes," he murmured.

When they got to the door, she opened it and looked out and then nodded to him. He had to make her stop twice on the way to the elevator to get his strength back.

On the way down he leaned against her and closed his eyes.

She shook him off.

"No, Gil. No. You'll drop to the floor this way. Open

your eyes. Try to keep holding on. Till I get you into my car."

"Okay," he muttered.

He forced his eyes open again.

"Okay," he muttered again.

The burst of wind upon his hot, fevered face almost exhilarated him. Then the pain took over again and he leaned against her each step of the way through the dark street till they came to her car.

He leaned like a drunk, heavily against the side of her car, while she took out her keys and opened the door. Then she helped him in, shut the door and dashed out into the night street to the other side of the car, opened the door and got in. A truck sped by, almost hitting the closing door, and the driver shouted at her and then his angry voice was carried away by the wind.

Now the street was silent again.

She turned on the motor, and he found himself listening to its hum, and then his eyes closed again and he drifted off.

He dreamed of the Dwarf.

They were standing in the well of the night in front of the tree. A small lantern gleamed at their side.

Gil had a shovel in his right hand.

"Dig, Gil. Dig."

"You sure you want me to?"

"Just dig and don't ask questions."

"But why?"

"Do as I tell you."

The Dwarf's voice was harsh and commanding.

"The box isn't there anymore."

"I know it isn't there, Gil."

"Somebody's stolen it."

"Gordie has it now. Our dear friend Gordie."

"Then why should I dig?"

"Because I tell you. I'm your big brother. That's why."

Gil turned furiously on him.

"You're not my big brother. Don't say the word *big* to me again. You're small and you're ugly and you're an evil Dwarf."

The Dwarf smiled, a cruel smile.

"Dig."

"Evil."

The Dwarf nodded his big head. His black eyes flashed.

"Good. Now you know the truth."

"You were always evil."

"Always. Dig."

He began digging and the Dwarf began to laugh.

Harshly.

Mockingly.

Gil stopped digging.

"Why are you laughing?"

"Because."

"Because what?"

"Because you're digging your own grave. That's what."

The shovel fell from Gil's hands and clattered.

The Dwarf's mad laughter became louder.

Gil thrust his hands to his ears.

"Stop it," he shouted. "Please stop it. I can't bear anymore."

But the wild brutal laughter rose and rose till it overwhelmed Gil and then he opened his eyes and it was the low voice of Casey that he heard.

"We're here, Gil."

"Where?"

He looked dazedly about him and saw rows of parked cars under overhead lights. He stared at the cement floor and concrete walls.

"We're on the top floor of a garage, Gil."

"I don't get it."

"We're leaving the car here and going out onto the roof."

"Why?"

She smiled gently at him.

"Come on. Trust me. You'll see what I mean."

She opened the door at his side.

"We can take our time now. Nobody comes up here. These are storage cars."

She slowly and tenderly helped him out of the car.

"Now we have to go to that door. Okay?"

"Uh-huh."

When they got to the metal door, she opened it with a key and they went through the doorway and onto the roof of the garage.

The wind blew down on them from the dark, starless sky.

Then Gil saw the outlines of a small shack and the glint of a window pane. A sharp beam of light suddenly hit the glass softly and he trembled as if it had hit him. Then he slowly realized that it came from her flashlight.

He leaned against an iron post as she let the beam play over the rest of the wooden shack.

"It's my hideaway," she said.

He looked at her.

"Nobody knows about it except my brother. He owns this garage. I come here when I want to get away from things."

"Gordie?"

She shook her head.

"Doesn't even know it exists."

He felt the night air soothe him. The pain was not so intense out there in the sweep of the cold wind.

He could almost stand without her help.

"Let's go in and you'll lie down again."

He waved his hand.

"Just another minute out here."

"All right."

"It's good for me."

"Sure. Whatever you want."

He looked away from her and into the reach of the

night. At the end of the roof he could see the iron railing of a fire escape that led down to the street.

He breathed in the cold air and even though his ribs cried out in pain with each movement of his chest he still went on with the breathing.

In deeply and out again.

I'll pull out of this fast, he said to himself.

My strength will come back and I'll be myself again.

And then I'll see what I can do.

That ape didn't break me.

I must always remember that.

He didn't break me.

"All right, Casey," he said.

He straightened up again and she put her arm about him and as she did he found himself wondering about her. She was so slightly built and yet she had been able to hold him up and get him here.

Where did her strength come from?

Where?

It's so hard to tell the truth about her, he thought.

She seems to be so full of contradictions.

They went through the doorway of the shack and he said to himself bitterly, It's so hard to tell the truth about anybody in this dark, twisted world of ours.

We all lie to each other.

All of us.

We put on masks all the time.

Who of us is the lord and owner of his own face?

Who?

Isn't that what Shakespeare pointed out in one of his sonnets?

We discussed it in one of the literature classes and Mr. Walden thought I was brilliant.

Brilliant in an English literature class.

How far, far away that is to me now.

"How do you like it, Gil?"

The room was small and cozy, and in one of its neat

corners he saw an easel and an unfinished canvas standing on its ledge.

She helped him to a couch and he sat down on it and then he decided to lie back and she came over with a blanket and covered him.

"Better?"

"Yes."

He pointed to the easel.

"Yours?"

"Oh. I play around with paint."

"Looks pretty good from here."

"You like art?"

"My aunt took me to museums. I got to enjoy going there."

"You still go?"

He nodded.

"Still."

"You'd come in to New York?"

"The Met and the other ones."

She went over to the canvas. It was a still life and its colors were bright and sure and glowing, the brush strokes soft and clean.

"I'm better with landscapes. I mean I feel better doing them."

"Why?"

"I guess it's because I come from a mining town. Lots of rain and mud and slag heaps. So I like to do glowing fields and splashes of sun and blue sky. I'm a fool."

She had said the last words softly and sadly.

"How long have you been at it?"

"Years. Too many years."

"And?"

"Just for kicks. Therapy."

He looked across the room to her and he shook his head.

"I don't believe you," he said. "You had your dreams. You still have them."

"No more."

She turned away from him and went over to a chair and slowly sat down. And as she did he saw how tired and worn she was.

A sudden feeling of pity and tenderness for her swept over him.

"What's going to happen to you?" he said.

"To me?"

"When Gordie finds out what you did."

She shrugged.

"I'll handle it."

"He'll start looking for you. The same as he's now looking for the Dwarf."

She shook her head.

"No. He won't start looking for me."

"How do you know that?"

"Because I'm going back to him now."

"What?"

"Yes, Gil. I'm leaving you here. You'll be safe."

He sat up even though the pain was still great.

"No, Casey. No. He'll . . ."

She cut in gently.

"He'll do nothing to me. I know Gordie too well."

"I don't believe you."

"You must. I'm going to make him see things my way."

"What is your way?"

"I told you. To see that the money is split evenly. Between Gordie and the Dwarf."

"You told me," he said coldly.

She got up and came over to him.

"Gil, listen to me. I'm leveling with you now."

"Are you?"

"Yes. Gordie lied to you. The Dwarf doesn't want all the money. He only wants his share."

"That's what the Dwarf said."

"He was telling the truth, Gil."

"Was he?"

"Yes."

He looked at her earnest face and he said to himself, and I was believing Gordie, beginning to believe him and to turn away from the Dwarf.

I called him in my heart, the lying Dwarf.

"It's the truth, Gil."

Even when Milo was beating me.

"I swear it to you. The truth."

The truth.

What is truth? Pontius Pilate asked and then did not wait for the answer.

Or did he?

Or did she?

Why did she stand there and let Gordie tell me lies?

Why?

"Why did you?"

"What do you mean, Gil?"

He forgot his pain. It was gone from him. Only his bitterness and anger remained.

"Why did you stand there and let Gordie tell me lies? I looked over to you and your face told me nothing. Nothing."

She paled and did not answer him.

"You said nothing. Not a single word."

She sighed low.

"I know that."

She looked old and tired to him. There were lines in her face that he did not see before.

Her blue eyes were clouded and dull.

"Well?"

He felt as if he was hitting her and yet he went on.

"Why did you do it? Why?"

She raised her head to him.

"I'm what I am, Gil."

"And what is that?"

"My father threw me out when I was sixteen. You take it from there."

He looked at her and didn't say anything.

"I wasn't completely on your side then, Gil. Not then," she said.

Are you now, Casey?

Are you?

"But Milo started to work on you and I . . . I . . . I just couldn't . . . ."

Her voice choked up and she couldn't go on.

He sat there looking at her and then away to the dark window and the night that lay beyond it.

The vast autumn night.

Cold and indifferent.

Ah, what do I want from her? he said to himself. Why don't I leave her alone? She saved my life and here I'm . . .

He heard her voice again.

"Trust me, Gil. And it will work out. Just trust me."

Her eyes pleaded with him.

"Will you, Gil?"

"Should I?" he asked in a harsh voice.

"Yes, Gil. Yes."

She sat down on the couch by him. He felt her closeness.

"I won't let you down."

She touched his hand gently and her touch was cold, so very cold.

"I won't. I promise you that."

And he said to himself, how many times have you said those words, Casey? And to how many people?

How many times have you lied to yourself?

"You have to believe me, Gil."

"I guess I have to," he said.

"You don't."

She looked at him with a haunting sadness in her eyes and then she slowly rose and went away from him.

"I'm going to Gordie. I'll be back sometime in the morning."

Will you?

"Try to sleep when I'm gone. No one will harm you here."

"Casey," he said.

She turned at the doorway.

"Yes?"

"Take care of yourself."

He saw her standing against the windy night, the light still on her face.

He could see the sadness in her eyes.

Still there.

The lost, lost sadness.

"Take care," he said again.

Then he saw her go through the doorway and the door closed.

13

The spatter of gravel against the window made him open his eyes. Then he heard the door open slowly and he sat up.

The wind came softly into the room and with it the sound of heavy, measured footsteps.

Then he saw the face come closer and closer to him.

The eyes black and flashing.

Little spits of fire coming out of them.

"Gil."

It was the Dwarf.

His brother the Dwarf.

"You all right?"

Gil just sat there gazing at him.

"They gave you a rough time, didn't they?"

"Yes."

"It's my fault. All my fault."

"It happened."

The Dwarf shook his big head.

"Because I made it happen. Listen to me."

The face in the night dimness was tight and fierce.

"Don't trust her, Gil."

"What do you mean?"

"She double crossed me. How do you think she knows you have the ticket?"

"She doesn't know I have it. She thinks I know where it is."

"Look at me."

And as he looked, he saw the little spits of fire come again from the Dwarf's black, black eyes.

"Listen to me."

He trembled with a great fear.

And then he heard the Dwarf's low and harsh voice again.

"She knows you have it. Because I told her."

"What?"

"That's how Milo knew you were on the train coming in to see me. I told her."

"So it was you?"

The Dwarf nodded his head.

"Yes. I thought she was my friend. That's how she is. It's good I didn't tell her the whole truth. Where the ticket really is. It's good I didn't do it."

The face moved back into the darkness, just a bit.

Yet Gil could still see the burning eyes.

"She gets to be your friend. She's a master at that."

She is, Gil thought bitterly.

"I used to tell her everything. Only her. Nobody else. And then she went and double crossed me."

He almost shouted the last words.

Gil was silent.

The Dwarf came out of the darkness and closer to him again.

"Don't trust her. And don't go to the police."

"Why not?"

"Listen to me."

"I don't understand. Why not?"

"Because you have nothing to go with. Gordie will frame you. You'll end up losing. Believe me, I know."

"I still don't get it."

"You don't have to. Just stay away from them."

Gil leaned forward to his brother.

"Then what am I supposed to do?"

And it seemed to him that as he said that, the walls of the room began to dissolve into the night and he could feel the wind blowing about him.

Chilling him to the bone.

"What are you supposed to do, Gil?"

"Tell me," he pleaded.

"You're asking me? Me?"

"Tell me, Gareth."

"I warned you never to call me Gareth."

"Tell me."

"Never."

"Why? Why not?"

"Because I'm an evil Dwarf."

And suddenly the Dwarf began to laugh and laugh and then, before Gil's eyes, he vanished into the blowing darkness and Gil knew that he had been dreaming.

A bitter, hopeless dream.

14

He went slowly across the roof and with each step upon the cold gravel he felt his strength returning to him. He came to the iron railing of the fire escape and he paused.

He looked at his watch.

It was one minute after midnight.

I've got to see the Dwarf, he said to himself. She lied to me. I know she did. He's still there in his cave. That's where he'd be safest. They couldn't get in to touch him there.

I'll be all right on the streets now. I'll be able to make my way to the Dwarf without Milo or Gordie seeing me.

This is the time to do it.

He went down the escape, step by step, slowly, as quietly as he could. His hand gripped the railing tightly.

He still felt flashes of pain, but they were bearable.

"I'll make it," he said in a low, hard voice.

And I'll beat them.

I'll bet my life I will.

And if I lose, I lose.

He swung down from the last bar of the fire escape and onto the hard dirt of the empty lot. Then he stood there, the wind blowing his hair about, till he got his bearings and then he started off again.

The garage lay close to the river and now he walked

along the silent dock streets, hugging close to the walls of the buildings. The only sound came from the passing trucks.

Then stillness again.

And in that stillness he heard the mournful whistle of a boat far out in the river, mournful and piercing.

A police car passed by, cruising slowly, and he felt a sudden impulse to call out to it, but he found his lips pressed tightly together.

The car was gone.

He stopped for an instant outside a bar just to listen to the pleasant talk of people inside and the low background sound of gentle music.

It warmed him.

They're enjoying themselves in there, he thought to himself. Away from the wind and the night. Just sitting around and drinking some beers and Irish whiskey and enjoying each other.

A neighborhood tavern.

People who know each other a long time.

Know and like each other.

And then he said to himself with a cry, Why are people so cruel to each other? Why, Casey?

Why can't we be happy with each other?

Why do we do the brutal things that we do to each other?

Casey?

Why?

He turned away from the tavern and went swiftly up the block, his hands slack at his side and his face bleak.

Soon he left the dock streets and went into the loft area. Now as he walked along he became alert and tense, watching every person who neared him with sharp, penetrating eyes, ready to move or dart away into the cover of darkness.

I've got to be careful, he said to himself.

Very careful.

Especially now that I'm on the Dwarf's block.

The street was deserted and still, and all he could see was the dark fronts of the gray amorphous buildings and the pools of light cast from the high lampposts onto the black pavement.

He went down the block, from light into darkness and then into a pool of shining light again, his blond hair becoming white and then gray again.

He stopped at 32.

One of the glorious winning numbers, he thought to himself wryly.

Dwarf, what have you really won?

Tell me.

What?

Gil went inside the building and into the creaky elevator and then up to the top floor. And as the old elevator rose, floor by floor, he felt the tension grow and boil within him.

His palms beginning to sweat.

His fingers to tremble.

I've got to hold on, he said to himself.

Hold on or I'm lost.

The elevator stopped and the door opened slowly.

He stuck his head out and cautiously searched the dim corridor to see if anybody was standing there in the shadows.

Standing and waiting to leap upon him.

He thought he saw the figure of Milo, hard against the wall.

He gasped and froze.

And then he realized that no one was there.

No one.

But shadows.

"Easy," he muttered low. "Take it easy."

He stepped out with a sigh.

Then he looked again into the shadows, turned and began to walk down the corridor to the Dwarf's door.

All the time imagining somebody silent, with great stealth, following closely behind him.

Until he could swear he could feel the breathing of the man on the nape of his neck.

A cold breath.

The chilling breath of Milo.

He stopped and swung about sharply, his hands clenched into fists, but no one was there.

Only the dim emptiness.

He came to the door and knocked.

The sound was loud against the stillness.

"Dwarf."

He waited and knocked again.

"Dwarf, it's Gil."

But no one came to the door.

Maybe she didn't lie to me, he thought.

Maybe he really did go into hiding.

"Dwarf."

He knocked again and again.

"Open up."

Then with anger and fear unsettling him, he put his hand to the knob and twisted it and rattled it. Suddenly the door swung open slowly.

He stood there motionless.

For there was no one waiting for him on the threshold.

Only the darkness.

And beyond the darkness the soft glow of a lamp.

His hand fell away from the knob and he realized that the door had been unlocked all the time.

A surge of terror swept over him and he turned to run to the elevator which was still there.

No, he said to himself. No.

He forced himself to go inside, down the dark hallway and straight to the glow of the lamp. And all the time his heart was pounding within him.

He stepped within the circle of light and it was then that he saw the small figure sitting on one of the small chairs in the room.

Sitting and gazing out the window and into the bleak night.

Gil went over to the Dwarf.

And saw that he was dead.

15

He was on his knees, looking into the staring eyes of the Dwarf, when he heard the distant sound of the elevator as it began to descend.

Gil rose to his feet and stood there listening intently.

Somebody's coming up here, he thought to himself.

I'm sure of it.

It's here.

They're coming here.

He went quickly to the front door and shut it quietly, making sure to leave it as he had found it.

Unlocked.

Then he went back and began searching desperately for a hiding place. All the time his eyes were going across the room to the small, silent figure staring with dead sight into the cold darkness.

They killed you, Dwarf, he said bitterly.

Killed you for the money.

Always the money.

He opened the closet door and he saw the Dwarf's clothes, small and neat, in rows on hangers and it was then that he felt the tears well up to his eyes.

For the clothes were like the clothes of a child.

Not those of an evil Dwarf.

Gareth, he thought. Gareth.

And it was at that instant that he heard dimly, very dimly, the sound of the elevator coming close to his floor.

He turned swiftly and ran down the hallway to the apartment door and stood there looking through the peephole and listening tensely. . . .

to the sound of the elevator.

Slowly, creakily, the elevator made its way up, up, till it stopped with a soft thud at his floor.

He trembled.

Then he saw the door open and the figures, first of Milo and then the lean dark shadow of Gordie.

He turned and ran swiftly down the hallway and into the shelter of the closet and then he closed the door, leaving but a thin opening for him to peer through.

He waited.

He heard the door slowly open and shut slowly and quietly.

The footsteps along the hallway.

Then he saw them come into the room and stop. Their shadows were ragged against the wall.

Gordie went silently over to the Dwarf and stood there looking down at him, a cold hard look in his brown eyes.

"He's dead, all right."

Milo didn't speak.

"Why did you do it?"

Milo didn't answer.

Gordie walked away from the dead man and stood there gazing through the window. His lean figure was taut with anger.

"Why?"

"I didn't mean to, Gordie."

"I sent you here to bring him to me. Not to kill him," Gordie said without turning.

"I told you I just . . . I really took it easy with him."

"Easy."

"I did. Honest, I did."

"You're only an ape. Casey was right."

"He put up too much of a fight. He was like a cat."

Gordie turned to him.

"Didn't you tell him I was ready to make a deal with him? A better deal? One he could go along with? Didn't you tell him that?

Milo moved back.

"Honest, I did, Gordie."

"You're lying."

"No. It's the truth. Just what you said. Casey could tell you that I . . ."

"Leave Casey out of this," Gordie said coldly.

"But . . ."

"I said leave her out of this."

"Sure, Gordie."

Gordie went over to the Dwarf again and stood there, looking down at him, his face impassive.

Yet Gil thought he could see a look of pain in his eyes.

Of pain and sorrow.

"Let's get him out of here."

Milo nodded silently.

"You'll pick him up and carry him."

"Yes, Gordie."

Milo bent over the small, silent figure.

"Wait a minute."

"Yes?"

Milo straightened up again.

"Better get his coat out of the closet. You'll cover him with it."

"All right."

He turned and started for the closet.

Gil froze and an icy sweat broke out all over him. He moved back as far as he could till he felt the cold, hard wall against him.

The door of the closet began to open.

I'm trapped, Gil said to himself desperately.

Now they'll surely kill me.

They'll take me and . . .

Suddenly he heard Gordie's voice.

"Milo."

The door stopped opening.

"What is it?"

"Get a blanket from the other room. That'll do the job better."

"Okay, Gordie."

Milo's voice moved away from Gil.

"Make it fast."

"Sure thing, Gordie."

And then the silence rushed in again.

Gil waited and then he slowly moved away from the wall and over to the cover of the half-opened door.

He stood in the sheltering darkness of the closet and looked out.

"How's this?"

Milo had come back into the room, carrying a small blanket in his big hands. Gil felt a sudden mad impulse to run out and tear the blanket from the murdering hands . . . the blanket that had been so close to his brother's body . . .

"Wrap it around him. And then pick him up and carry him against your shoulder."

"Right."

"Like you're carrying a big sleeping child."

"He's sleeping."

"Shut up."

Milo picked up the Dwarf and Gordie came over and arranged the blanket over the little dead man's face.

Gil thought he could see Gordie's hands shaking.

But he couldn't be sure.

"Carry him out to the car and put him on the back seat."

"How about the trunk?"

"Only if the street is clean."

"Nobody's there now."

"Just make sure. Remember."

Milo nodded.

"Where are we taking him, Gordie?"

"Where nobody will ever find him again."

"The river?"

"Yes. You should know the spot. You've been there before."

Milo grinned.

"I have. He never liked water."

"He'll like it now," Gordie said in a flat voice.

"What do we do with the kid?"

"His brother?"

"What's the next move with him?"

"I'll tell you when I decide. Get going."

"Okay."

"I'll stay up here a minute or two."

Gil heard Milo's heavy footsteps go down the hallway and then he heard the door open and close.

All became still again.

Gil could hear the soft somber sound of the wind against the window. He saw Gordie stand there looking down at the small empty chair and listening to the bleak wind.

His face impassive, the brown eyes veiled.

Then Gil saw Gordie go slowly over to the Velasquez that hung on the far wall of the shadowed room.

Las Meninas.

And the words his brother had spoken to Gil came back to him. I was born in the wrong century, Gil. This century is too cruel and too heartless to its weak and its crippled. And I'm really a cripple in their eyes. Worse than a cripple. A freak. A circus freak who has no circus.

The wrong century, Gil.

So very wrong.

All the centuries were wrong to you, Gareth, Gil said in his aching bitterness.

All of them, Dwarf.

Through his tears he saw Gordie looking long at the little Dwarf lady, Mari Barbella.

Her soft glowing eyes.

So gentle and compassionate.

Then Gil heard the man say in a very low voice.

"You never did get to marry her, did you, Dwarf?"

The words faded away into the shadows.

Then Gil saw Gordie turn and go out of view, and soon he heard the footsteps down the hallway.

The door shut.

After that the silence came in again.

The silence and the wind.

16

He was walking down the dark, windy street when the car pulled up alongside him and he heard the voice.

"Gil."

It was Casey.

"Get in. Get in quick."

He turned to go away from her, but she got out of the car and came over to him.

"Listen to me. Please."

"No."

She put her hand out to him and he pushed it away.

"Gil."

"I don't want to listen to anything."

"You have to."

He shook his head fiercely.

"I'm going to the police. Once and for all."

"Don't do it."

"It's just down the block. And you're not stopping me. Nobody is."

"You'll only make things worse."

"They can't be any worse."

"You don't understand."

"Leave me alone."

He started away from her again.

Then he heard her call out.

"They'll kill your aunt."

He stopped and stared at her.

"What?"

"Is that what you want?"

"No."

"They'll do it. Believe me they will."

Her face was white and taut.

"They killed the Dwarf," he said tonelessly.

"I know."

"They killed him."

"And if you go to the police can you prove that it was Gordie and Milo who did it? Can you?"

He didn't answer.

"Can you even prove that he's dead?"

"I saw him dead."

"You saw him. But where is the Dwarf now? Where?"

In the river, he said to himself hopelessly.

Go find him in the river.

The river.

The muddy, dirty river.

He looked at Casey and felt like weeping.

"Gil, it's your word. Only a word."

"My word," he murmured.

"They've got you beaten. Don't you see that?"

"It's not right," he said. "Not right."

"When were things right in this world? When?"

When? he echoed.

He stood there with the night wind blowing against him and then he turned away from her and bowed his head.

She came close to him.

"Gil, come with me."

He didn't speak.

"Please. I begged you to trust me. You must. It's your only hope now."

"What do you want?"

"Come into the car."

He stood there, not moving.

"Please, Gil. You've got nowhere else to go."
He shrugged wearily.
"You're safe with me."
Am I? he thought and didn't care anymore.
"I promise you that."
She opened the door and he got in silently.
"That's better," she said gently.
Then she got in on her side and started up the motor.
"Just trust me, Gil," she said.
He was silent.

17

They were riding along the West Side Highway when she spoke to him again.

"Gil, my purse is right between us. Open it."

"Why?"

"Just do it."

He picked up the purse and opened it.

"There's a small wallet and a gun."

"What?"

"Don't touch the gun. Just take out the wallet."

His hand moved away from the cold barrel of the gun and found the small leather wallet.

He took it out.

"Open it."

"Well?"

"Switch on the dome light and take a look at what is in it."

He turned on the dome light.

"What do you see?"

He couldn't speak.

"It's Gordie's half of the ticket," she said.

"His half," he whispered.

He held it in his hand and checked the numbers.

She was right.

This and the Dwarf's half . . .

Six million dollars.

He put the ticket back into the wallet and the wallet back into the purse and clicked it shut.

Then he set the purse down next to her again.

All the time he was aware of her eyes checking every move he made.

"Now don't ask me questions. Let me do the speaking."

He waited.

"I have one half of the ticket. You know where the other half is. And don't ask me how I know."

He stared into the night ahead of him.

"Gil, I want you to take me to the other half."

"Why?"

"Because it's the only way left for you. You'll save your life and your aunt's."

He turned to her.

"How will that happen?"

She slowed the car down.

"Once we have the full ticket we're in the clear. We go down the first thing in the morning to the lottery office and register the ticket in both our names."

"Both?"

"Yes."

"And then?"

"The six million belongs to both of us. Gordie can't touch it anymore. He's lost."

"Lost?" Gil said bitterly. "Gordie never loses."

She pulled the car over to the shoulder of the road and shut off the motor.

"I'll take care of Gordie. I'll give him what I decide is his share. I had him seeing things my way and then Milo ruined everything."

They were silent.

"Gil, take me to the ticket. Listen. I'm the only one who can save you from Gordie. The only one. He'll never let you go. Your life is not worth a nickel without me. He'll get to you and kill you. I'm the only one who can save you now. Do it my way. I tell you I'll handle him when I give him his share. He listens to me."

"I have some questions," Gil said.

She shook her head.

"I know them. When this is all over I'll give you the answers. Until then you've got to trust me."

"How do I know you won't double cross me?"

She looked at him and her eyes were large and cold. "You don't."

"So?"

"So you trust me. What else is there for you to do? Tell me."

He didn't answer her.

He sat there listening to the cars go by him, one after another, one after another, endlessly.

Their lights, like blind white eyes, searching the night.

And he said to himself, she's right.

What else can I do?

"Well?"

He turned to her.

"All right," he said. "You win."

"I thought I would."

"You were sure of it, weren't you?"

"I was, Gil."

And as she said those words, he felt the gun barrel pressed hard into his side.

He trembled and stared at her.

"What is . . . ?"

It was all done so suddenly, so deliberately and so skillfully.

"Gil," she said. "I could just as well have tried it this way, couldn't I? Forced you with a gun to take me there? But I didn't. Did I?"

He couldn't speak.

"I talked to you," she said.

She took the gun away from his side and dropped it into her purse and then set the purse down on the seat between them.

''Now do you believe me?''

He slowly nodded.

''Good,'' she said softly and smiled at him.

Then she started up the motor again and drove the car back onto the highway.

''Let's go for that six million. Right, Gil?''

The car sped off into the night.

18

They had stopped for some gas and to get some coffee. She left him alone at the table for a long while, and he sat there thinking of the Dwarf.

He fought like a cat, Milo said.

Like a wildcat.

And the memory came back to Gil of the time he was going to school. It was his freshman year, and Ed Bradley, a big lineman on the school football team, for some hidden, twisted reason used to wait for Gil every morning and badger and bully him.

Morning after bitter morning, until Gil could take it no longer and tried to fight him, but it was no match and soon he was on the ground stunned and beaten.

And as he was lying there, feeling ashamed and hopeless, he suddenly heard a hoarse shout and then he saw a body fling itself on Ed Bradley with a savage fury. It was the Dwarf. He kicked and bit and scratched away until Bradley backed off and turned and left them.

Glad to get away.

"Get up, Gil."

Gil slowly rose to his feet and looked down at his brother.

"He hurt you much?"

"No."

"You've got to fight the bullies of this life," the Dwarf said.

"I tried to."

"Then you try again. No matter how big and tough they are."

"But you fought them and they killed you. They went and killed you and dumped you into the dirty river."

The Dwarf shook his head grimly.

His black eyes flashed.

"I'm still living. You haven't forgotten me. You'll never forget me. I'm still living."

"I'm still living," Gil echoed softly, his heart aching.

And he looked up and saw Casey standing at the table staring at him.

"What is it, Gil?"

"Nothing."

"Tell me."

"I was thinking of the Dwarf," he said in a low voice.

"Oh."

"Why did they have to kill him?"

"Let's go," she said. "We've been here too long."

He got up and followed her out to the car.

19

But when they got to the car, it wouldn't start.

It took almost two hours before they were able to get onto the highway again.

"Somebody up there is trying to block us out, Gil," she said. "It's always been that way with me."

Then she pressed her foot down hard on the accelerator.

"This time nothing is stopping me. Nothing."

He looked at her taut profile and then thought of the gun lying in her purse.

Nothing will, he said to himself.

20

The lamp was on in the front window.

The rest of the house was dark.

Joe is sound asleep, he thought. Knocked out from the long day at the store. Aunt Edith is lying in bed next to him, her eyes open, staring at the dark ceiling and thinking about me.

And the Dwarf.

He looked up at the silent windows and then he walked down the long driveway, slowly, noiselessly, until he came to the garage. He quietly opened the door and went inside and found the lantern and the small shovel where he had left them.

The dirt was still caked on the gleaming blade of the shovel.

He went out of the garage, closing the door carefully and silently.

Then he walked down the deserted moonless road to where the car was parked under the shelter of a large tree.

"You've got them?"

He stood listening to the low sound of the wind before answering her.

The wind going through the leafless branches.

"Yes," he said.

"Let's go."

He opened the door and got into the car beside her.

"About two miles down?"

"Yes," he said.

"There's an old empty barn. And the tree."

He nodded.

She was driving slowly along the road.

"Why is the lamp on in the house?"

"It's that way every night," he said.

"Why?"

And he wanted to say that he didn't know, but suddenly he did know.

"She keeps it on for the Dwarf," he said.

"Your aunt?"

"Yes. Ever since he left the house."

"She must have loved him."

"In her way."

They drove along into the night and the thrust of the low wind.

"I loved him, too," Casey said. "In my way."

21

All the time he was digging he felt the Dwarf standing there just under the dark, lonely branches of the elm tree, standing there, the shine of the lantern barely reaching him.

Standing there and watching Gil.

His black eyes large, fierce and glowing.

And Gil could swear he could hear his low, harsh voice speaking in cold rhythm with each stroke of the shovel.

Stop digging, Gil.

Stop it.

You're digging your grave.

Leave the box where it is, Gil.

Stop digging.

Don't trust her.

She's a killer.

He paused and still he heard the Dwarf's voice.

At the diner, she went to the phone to call them and tell them where you were going. That's why she left you sitting at the table so long.

Don't trust her.

There was nothing wrong with the car. She set it all up with the gas station guy. Didn't you see the look that passed between them? She must have paid him off to go along with the scam.

She was stalling for time.

Don't trust her.

Gil began digging again.

You'll find the ticket, all right.

But listen to me, Gil.

Listen to me.

It is a death ticket.

That's what it really was all the time.

A death ticket.

Gil!

His shovel touched the top of the box and he paused and straightened up and looked over to the woman.

Her eyes were glowing.

"Is that the box?" she whispered.

She suddenly looked old to him, so very old.

He nodded silently.

"Get it."

He knelt down onto the ground and lifted the box out of the hole and held it in his hands.

His fingers traced along the embossed figure of the frog.

"Open it," Casey said.

He opened the box and took out the ticket.

"Yes," she whispered as she saw it.

She knelt at his side.

"Now we have it. Just you and I, Gil."

He didn't say anything.

She rose and then he heard the click of her purse opening and a sudden wave of terror swept over him and he waited for the cold barrel of the gun to point at his head.

But it was the wallet that she took out.

"Give me the ticket, Gil."

He rose and silently handed it over to her.

"It will be safe here," she said.

And she put the Dwarf's half next to Gordie's half and stood there gazing at the full ticket.

"It looks so beautiful," she said. "Six million dollars of beauty."

And it was then that he thought he could hear the sound of the Dwarf's sad laughter, a distant, thin sound that was lost in the wind.

Gil turned sharply and saw the two figures slide out of the darkness of the old barn and slowly approach the light of the lantern.

His heart tightened within him.

His hands became cold and they trembled.

It was Gordie and Milo.

The Dwarf was right, he thought bitterly. I've dug my own grave.

Gordie came over to them, the lantern light on his face, his shadow lean and sharp on the hard ground.

Milo moved over to the other side of Gil.

He stood there leaning against the tree.

Stood there and loomed.

"You've got it," Gordie said to Casey.

She nodded, but her eyes were on Milo, cold and appraising.

"My way was the right way," she said. "All the time, Gordie."

"Let's finish this off and get going."

She turned back to Gordie.

"There's nothing to finish off," she said quietly.

"What do you mean?"

"We've got the ticket. That's all we need."

Gordie shook his head coldly.

"He's too dangerous to be left this way."

"That was the deal. Gil was not to be touched."

"No good, Casey."

"I said he's not to be touched. Go to the car, Gil."

Gordie silently pushed her aside and motioned to Milo.

"Do it and do it fast."

Gil raised his hands to fight off the big man, but then

he felt a jarring blow on his cheek and he staggered back.

Then he felt Milo's steel fingers begin to close about his neck and he began to gasp for breath and just as darkness was rushing in over him he heard the dim voice of Casey.

"Stop it, Milo. Stop it."

The sound of a gun.

"Casey," Gordie shouted.

The hands about his neck slowly relaxed their hold and then he saw in a haze the big man sink down and away from him.

Gil breathed in the night air.

"Gil."

Casey was standing by him, her gun in her hand.

"Go to the car and start the motor. Quick."

She pushed him hard and he began to run and it was then that he heard the two shots, in quick succession.

He stopped stock still and slowly turned and saw Casey move back and stand against the elm tree.

Her face was white and slack.

He saw Gordie lying flat on the ground, his gun at his side.

"Casey."

He came up to her.

"Pick up my purse," she said.

He stared at her.

"Do it."

He knelt and picked up her purse.

"Now you'd better help me to the car," she said.

Her hand was over her breast and there was blood dripping onto it.

"I always end up a loser," she said.

22

He was going to take her to the Milburn hospital, but she made him pull over to the side of the road.

"I feel better this way."

He sat there listening to the wind, his eyes away from her.

"I'm not going to make it, Gil," she said.

He didn't turn to her.

"Why should you care? Why should anybody care?"

He bowed his head.

"I double crossed you. I double crossed the Dwarf. In the end I double crossed myself."

"Maybe it's better you don't talk, Casey," he said.

She shook her head.

"Doesn't make any difference anymore."

He started up the motor.

"I'm going on to the hospital."

She put her hand gently on his.

"Please, Gil. It's too much pain that way."

He turned off the motor again.

The sound of the wind came in to them.

"You hate me, don't you?" she said, and her voice was getting lower.

He shook his head.

"You should, Gil."

"No," he said.

"I didn't mean for the Dwarf to be killed. It happened before I could do anything. You have to believe me."

She began to cough and he waited for her to stop.

"I do believe you," he said.

He saw the tears in her eyes and he clenched his hands tight.

"He loved you, Gil. He was such a good and decent human being. You never knew him as I did. He loved you with all his great soul."

Gil turned away from her.

There was a long silence.

When he turned back to her again, she was dead.

23

He sat there a long time and then he picked up her purse and opened it and took out the wallet and then the ticket.

He held the ticket in his hand.

A drop of her blood had fallen on it.

And as he looked at the small clotted drop of blood, he could hear the voice of the Dwarf.

The sad, sad voice.

It was a death ticket, wasn't it, Gil?

"Yes."

He took the ticket and tore it into little bits and then he opened the car window and flung the bits out into the wind.

"Gareth," he whispered.

And then again, "Gareth."

He turned on the motor and then drove the car back onto the road and headed it for the town police station.

JAY BENNETT has won, in two successive years, The Mystery Writers of America's Award for the "best juvenile mystery." The author of many suspense novels for young adults, Mr. Bennett has also written successful adult novels, stage plays, and radio and television scripts.

Mr. Bennett's professed aim in his young adult novels (which have sold over three million copies) is "to write honest books that speak about violent times . . . but throughout the books, and in every word I write, there is a cry against violence."